Daffodils and Devon Scones

NETTLES B&B PARA COZY

BOOK FOUR

CHRISSY CHICORY

HALF-PAST 2 PUBLISHING INC.

ISBN (Print- Amazon): 978-1-963402-23-0

ISBN (Print- Draft2Digital): 978-1-963402-24-7

LCCN: 2026901784

Published by Half-Past 2 Publishing Inc.

Edited by Kimberly Huther

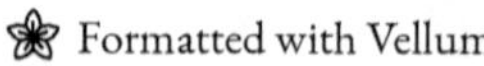

On my daily walks, I passed by the most enchanting place—the ***River Lily Inn****. Its beautiful façade captured my heart and quietly sparked the imagination that would grow into this series. This book is dedicated to* ***Mary****, the proprietress of the River Lily Inn, who kindly welcomed me and, as we walked the grounds together, showed me her heart-shaped pool—an image that lingered and eventually found its way into these pages.*

With gratitude for her warmth, generosity, and the gentle inspiration she so freely gave.
Chrissy

Contents

Prologue

The Cello That Dreamed
February 17, 1924

The fire had burned itself down to a bed of coals, the kind that glowed like watchful eyes in the grate. Each pulse of light threw long, wavering shadows across the parlor walls, making the room seem to breathe with the cold February night.

Cordelia knelt on the hearthrug, a burgundy wool shawl wrapped tight around her shoulders, her sensible day dress buttoned up to the throat. She tipped a few pieces of coal into the grate. Sparks flared, briefly illuminating her elegant, pale features—the long, fine-boned face; the straight, aristocratic nose; the cool, appraising eyes set beneath delicately arched brows. Her fair hair, pinned into rigid, orderly waves close to her head, gleamed briefly in the firelight before settling back into shadow. The determined line of her mouth tightened as the coal caught, casting her in a low amber glow.

Behind her, Bithia moved quietly around the tea tray, steam rising from the pot in delicate curls. Her midnight-blue shawl was draped over her dove-gray dress, the fringe brushing the floor as she crossed to the hearth. Firelight caught the gentle planes of her face—her fine, symmetrical features softening beneath the glow, her dark brows arching with their habitual, thoughtful poise. Her dark hair, parted neatly and swept into a controlled updo, gleamed like polished mahogany. There was a composure about her, a serene steadiness that made even her smallest movements feel intentional, almost ceremonial.

Even her fingertips were flushed pink from the chill. The house, for all its charms, had a talent for holding on to winter.

"Draft from the east window again," Cordelia murmured, pushing the poker into the coals. "If this house grows any more contrary, it will start giving me medical complaints."

Bithia smiled softly, the firelight catching in her eyes. "The spring bulbs will sprout soon."

Cordelia sank into her chair with a huff, though the fire's warmth eased some of her stiffness. "Well, that's a cheery thought."

They sat close to the hearth, the upright piano looming silently in the corner, its polished surface reflecting the flickering light in fractured gold. Outside, the Atlantic wind pressed against the windowpanes, carrying the scent of salt and the faint hum of the sleeping town.

On the table beside them laid the newspaper, creased and softened from use. Bithia reached for it, smoothing a page. "New York premiered a new musical work last week—*Rhapsody in Blue.* They say it sounds like a train, a storm, and a dream all at once."

Cordelia raised a brow. "Possibly all disasters."

"Possibly all wonders," Bithia countered gently. "Apparently the pianist played as though possessed. Imagine—music carried on the airwaves for all to hear."

Cordelia's gaze drifted to the wooden cabinet at the edge of the room. The wireless radio sat inside it like a brooding animal. They had only just learned how to coax sound from the thing.

"It gave us nothing but static earlier," Cordelia said. "And a man shouting sports scores."

"That was progress," Bithia replied with a small laugh.

She rose and crossed to the cabinet. Her fingers traced the radio's knobs with a cautious familiarity. When she turned one, the room filled with a thin, wavering hum. For a moment —just a heartbeat—music shimmered through the static. A bright flare of trumpet. A quick run of piano keys. Applause.

Then it dissolved into a long sigh of static.

Cordelia leaned forward. "Was that—?"

"New York, perhaps," Bithia said, adjusting the dial until the hum thinned to silence again.

She returned to her chair. The fire popped sharply, making both women start. The silence that followed settled with unusual weight.

Bithia wrapped her fingers around her teacup. "It feels different tonight," she murmured. "As though the house is waiting."

Cordelia didn't answer at once. The tension behind her breastbone had been quietly growing all evening. "Waiting for what?"

Bithia looked toward the dark hallway leading to the front door. The faintest draft curled along the floorboards.

"For someone," she said.

The mantel clock chimed the half hour—clear, deliberate, and too loud in the hush.

The house seemed to inhale.

Cordelia set down her cup. "I don't like that feeling."

Bithia folded her hands in her lap, steady and still. "Neither do I."

Footsteps did not approach. The wind did not rise. And yet—

Three soft knocks sounded at the door.

Measured. Intentional.

Both sisters lifted their heads at once.

The knock lingered in the air long after it had faded—a soft, hopeful tapping that felt strangely at odds with the cold February night.

Cordelia rose first, spine straight, expression arranged into polite neutrality. Bithia followed more slowly, smoothing her shawl as she moved down the hallway toward the front door. A faint draft curled along the floorboards, nipping their ankles.

When Bithia opened the door the winter air swept in, carrying with it the scent of rain-wet wood. A woman stood on the porch, her cloak dusted with travel grit and the hem darkened by coastal fog. She held a cello case in her left hand, and in her right a velvet-wrapped bow was pressed tightly to her chest.

"Ms. Croker?" the woman asked, breath clouding faintly in the cold. Her voice trembled—threaded with exhaustion yet softened by a New England lilt. "I hope I haven't called too late in the evening."

"Not at all," Bithia said gently. "Please, come in."

She stepped back to allow the visitor inside. The stranger hesitated only long enough to shift the bow more securely in her grip, as though even a moment's release might shatter something within her.

When she stepped into the parlor the flames brightened, casting her features into clearer view. She was pale—the pallor of sleepless nights rather than illness—but undeniably striking. Her dark hair was cut in a soft, chin-length bob, the fashionable style worn by artists and modern women from Boston to Paris. It framed her face in gentle waves, though the damp air had coaxed several wisps loose to cling to her cheeks.

Her hat, a modest felt cloche with a small appliqué bloom

on one side, sat askew from travel. Beneath its brim, her eyes appeared red-rimmed but steady—clear with purpose despite the grief hollowing their edges. Her mouth, though soft in shape, was pressed into a careful line, as if she were holding herself together by sheer will.

"Please," Bithia said, guiding her toward the nearest armchair. "Sit. Warm yourself."

Cordelia was already reaching for an extra shawl, which the woman accepted with a grateful nod. She set the cello case down with practiced reverence beside her knee, never letting it leave her immediate reach. Only after she had lowered herself into the chair did her grip loosen slightly on the bow.

"What is your name?" Cordelia asked, seating herself across the fire.

"Elena Volterra," she replied softly. "From Boston."

Cordelia's brows rose in surprise. "You've traveled quite a distance for an unannounced call."

Elena swallowed, eyes dropping to the cello case. "I didn't know where else to go."

Bithia poured tea into a clean cup, hands steady and sure. "Then you have come to the right place." She pressed the warm cup into Elena's trembling hands. "Drink. It will help."

Elena accepted the cup, though her fingers still shook. "Your names were in our newspaper back home," she said quietly. "Two weeks ago. After Mr. Houdini's visit."

Cordelia stiffened almost imperceptibly.

Elena continued, "He's made a career of exposing fraud. He discredits every medium he encounters. And yet..." Her voice thinned with awe. "He found no fault in your work. Not a single expose. Not a single accusation. He called your methods 'scrupulously precise'."

Bithia's expression softened with a kind of humility tinged by sadness. "Mr. Houdini is a man of... strong convictions."

"And a stronger skepticism," Cordelia added dryly.

Elena nodded. "Which is why I came. If he couldn't disprove you... I thought perhaps you might help me."

She tightened her grip on the bow.

On the small table between them, Bithia placed a plate of fresh biscuits left over from earlier in the day. Elena looked at them as though the concept of food was a distant memory.

"You must eat something," Bithia encouraged. "I insist."

Elena broke off a small piece and brought it to her lips. The warmth surprised her; her shoulders sagged a little as she exhaled. "Thank you," she whispered. "It's been... days. I can't seem to keep track."

Cordelia studied her with quiet scrutiny. "What brings you to us, Mrs. Volterra?"

The woman's gaze drifted to the bow wrapped in navy velvet. Her fingers tightened around it.

"My husband," she began, voice unsteady but determined. "Anton Volterra. He was a cellist."

Bithia and Cordelia exchanged a brief glance—both recognizing the fragile edge of the moment. Bithia nodded gently.

"When did you lose him?" she asked.

"Nine months ago." Elena inhaled shakily. "It feels like yesterday. Or a century. I... I can't seem to decide which."

She closed her eyes as though bracing herself. When she spoke again, the words came with the soft cadence of memory.

"I first heard him in a rehearsal room I wasn't supposed to be in. I was young, teaching piano lessons in a drafty little studio above a bakery in Boston. I pretended to be a page-turner for a visiting pianist just to hear the ensemble practice." A faint smile flickered. "Anton played like twilight in human form. Warm, steady; full of something I didn't have words for at the time."

Cordelia felt herself soften despite her best efforts.

"He asked me to accompany him at a small recital," Elena continued. "We argued about tempo for an hour and fell in love by the end of the week." She shook her head slightly. "Our romance moved faster than reason allowed. One season we were colleagues. The next, we were married and boarding steamships for Italy, Paris, Chicago—everywhere music would take us."

"And the instrument?" Bithia asked. "The case you brought. Is that his?"

Elena's expression gentled with reverence as her fingers brushed the navy velvet.

"La Dormiente," she whispered. "The Sleeping One. A cello crafted in 1891 by Carlo Giuliani. Anton said it resonated most beautifully in silence, as though the instrument preferred to be listened to closely." Her hand drifted to the case, tracing its worn edges. "Audiences used to say the cello had a soul."

"And the bow?" Cordelia asked. "You hold it as though it might fly away."

Elena swallowed. With careful fingers, she revealed a sliver of the bow beneath the velvet sleeve. The pernambuco wood gleamed richly even in the dim light. The silver-mounted frog caught the fire's glow. Just above it, a small oval of dark blue velvet had been stitched neatly into place.

"I embroidered this sleeve myself," Elena said. "And I added the thumb cushion when winter practice began to hurt his hand." Her voice thinned. "He used to say the bow felt warmer with it."

She drew a ragged breath.

"We toured through the influenza years," she said. "He grew tired, then thinner. His heart... it was never strong. But music kept him going. Always music."

The fire popped softly, as if punctuating her grief.

"One night, after a final performance in Boston," she whispered, "he fell asleep with the bow in his hand. Wrapped in this velvet." Her throat tightened. "I found him like that the next morning. Peaceful. As though mid-lullaby."

Neither sister spoke. Bithia's hand hovered motionless above her own teacup.

Elena lifted her gaze, eyes filled with memory threatening to escape through the tears gathering there. "I don't wish to disturb him. Or call him back. I wish only for one thing."

Bithia leaned forward, her voice barely above a breath. "And what is that, Mrs. Volterra?"

Elena pressed the bow to her heart.

"To know," she whispered, "that his music has not vanished from the world."

The parlor seemed to inhale with the three women still inside it. The fire quieted to a low murmur; even the draft beneath the east window felt suspended, as though the house were listening.

Bithia stood first.

"Elena," she said gently, "will you come sit with us at the séance table?"

Elena nodded. The velvet-wrapped bow trembled in her hands as she rose. She carried grief the way others carried lanterns—cupped close, shielding it from the wind.

Cordelia led the way, striking a match as they crossed the threshold into the séance corner. She lit the candles one by one, their thin flames lifting, trembling, then settling into a steady glow. Shadows slid up the walls, gathering in the corners like silent observers.

The table's lace-edged cloth was smoothed to perfect symmetry, the spirit board tucked beneath. Tonight, no planchette would be used. Tonight, something else had been invited.

Elena's breath shuddered as she set the cello case down on the floor beside her chair. Even closed, it seemed to gleam faintly in the low candlelight, its brass latches winking like half-lidded eyes. She rested her hand atop it, steadying herself.

Cordelia took the seat beside her, back straight, expression cool and inscrutable. But her gaze was sharp—too sharp—for someone who claimed to distrust séances entirely. She positioned one hand on the back of Bithia's chair, almost protectively.

Bithia sat last, folding her hands before her. Her dark eyes drifted to the velvet sleeve in Elena's grip.

"May I?" she asked.

Elena hesitated only a moment. Then she extended the bow—the fabric of the sleeve worn with years of touch. Bithia took it carefully, her fingertips grazing the soft pile.

A whisper of warmth traveled up her hand.

The candle flame nearest her steadied then rose a fraction higher, as though greeting an old acquaintance.

Cordelia's head snapped toward the candle.

"Bithia," she warned softly.

But Bithia was already elsewhere—not removed from the room, but drawn more fully into it. Her breath lengthened. Her shoulders eased. The hush gathered around her like a held chord.

The space beside her responded.

Light bent there, not dimming so much as redirecting, as if the air received a forming shape. The candle's glow stretched thin, passing through a figure that had no weight to cast a shadow yet altered everything it touched. The room adjusted its balance around him.

Anton Volterra had arrived.

He hovered just clear of the floorboards, held aloft as though the house had chosen not to insist upon his weight. His form gathered gradually, encouraged by the instrument rather than summoned by it—tall and spare, shaped by discipline and long hours of listening. Light traveled through him unevenly, lingering along the strong line of his shoulders and the fine planes of his face, passing cleanly through the softer edges.

He wore a dark wool suit, charcoal edged with blue, impeccably tailored and brushed smooth. The jacket sat close at the waist, the lapels narrow and precise. A crisp white shirt gleamed faintly beneath, its collar soft from use, and a silk tie —deep burgundy, knotted with practiced care—rested perfectly at his throat. Where the firelight crossed him the fabric caught a muted sheen, threads brightening and dimming.

His hair, thick and dark, curled gently at the temples, untouched by the draft that stirred the room. His face carried the marks of a man who had lived inwardly much more than outwardly: fine-boned, attentive, composed. Curiosity softened his expression now, easing the concentration that had once governed rehearsal halls and concert stages. His eyes—dark, reflective—moved first to the cello case then to the bow in Bithia's hands, taking in each detail with quiet recognition.

One hand hovered near the instrument, fingers curved in the familiar shape of readiness, never crossing the final distance. The other shaped the air unconsciously, tracing a tempo only he could hear. With each subtle motion the candle flame responded, lifting and narrowing, the light bending as though sound had taken on form.

He leaned closer, drawn by the resonance that lingered in the room. The cello answered with a faint, sympathetic vibration. Wood recognizing intention. Anton's mouth curved, not quite a smile but something warmer. Relief, perhaps, or gratitude.

He had found it.

And the room, adjusted by his presence, waited.

Bithia felt him before she turned her head. The nearness

pressed softly against her awareness. Her breath caught, then steadied.

"Oh," she whispered.

Cordelia stiffened. "What do you see?"

Bithia did not answer at once. She lifted her gaze, eyes reflecting more light than they should have held. When she spoke, her voice carried certainty rather than surprise.

"He is fully here," she said quietly.

Elena's breath broke in her chest. "Anton?"

The name moved through the room like a second melody.

Anton inclined his head. The motion sent a subtle ripple through the air, a shimmer that brushed Bithia's cheek. The candle flame leaned toward him, obedient.

"He listens," Bithia said, her voice softened by reverence. "As he always did."

She turned slightly, enough that Elena could follow her gaze. Not to see him, but to feel where the room held its attention.

"Elena," Bithia murmured, "did he love to practice at night?"

Elena pressed her hand to her mouth. Tears gathered, unbidden. "Every night," she said. "He said the world finally quieted enough to hear him."

Anton's fingers curved more fully then, shaping an unheard phrase. The cello answered with a faint, sympathetic hum.

Cordelia drew a sharp breath. She couldn't see him, but the air had shifted. The fire had stilled. The room leaned inward, attentive.

"This is no imagining," Cordelia said, her voice drawn taut as wire.

"No," Bithia agreed quietly.

Anton's gaze lifted then, moving between the three women as though taking attendance. His attention lingered first on Elena—on the bow clutched close to her chest, on the grief that had hollowed space for music to return. Then it passed to Cordelia, whose vigilance had sharpened into something weary. At last his eyes settled on Bithia.

Bithia inclined her head, acknowledgment rather than greeting. Her breath shifted—one clean intake, sudden and deep—as though her lungs had remembered an old instruction.

"Anton?" she asked, her tone measured. "Is it your desire to play once again?"

He answered by moving with unmistakable intention. He drifted to her side, the air responding to his nearness. His hand aligned over hers, close enough that warmth gathered there; close enough that memory found its way into muscle. The candle flame leaned. The cello case hummed softly in recognition.

Bithia's fingers obeyed, receiving the bow from Elena.

She loosened the velvet sleeve, the fabric whispering as it fell away. The bow emerged fully—pernambuco gleaming, silver-mounted frog catching a shard of firelight. The thumb cushion, sewn with patient care, rested exactly where it should.

A tremor of delight passed through Anton, subtle as a held breath.

Cordelia's hand tightened on the chair back. "Bithia," she said, restraint fraying, "I don't like this."

"It is all right," Bithia replied, her voice layered now—still her own, yet shaped by deeper current. "He wishes to play. And we are listening."

She rose, unhurried, her movements fluid, as though tempo had already been set. Anton stepped back half a pace, offering space with the courtesy of a man long accustomed to shared stages and narrow wings.

Elena covered her mouth. Tears escaped freely now, no longer held in check.

Inside the case, La Dormiente rested, varnish glowing like old amber. The cello bore the marks of long devotion—edges softened by hands, curves shaped by years of breath and bow. Bithia lifted it with practiced reverence, the instrument settling against her as though it had been waiting.

Cordelia's fear shifted, tempered by awe. "What has hold of you?" she murmured.

Bithia didn't answer. She had already taken her seat, the cello drawn between her knees with the ease of someone whose body remembered before the mind could interfere.

Anton moved closer.

His presence aligned behind her. His hand hovered above her shoulder, his posture mirroring hers exactly—spine lengthened, chin inclined, breath matched to hers. No shadow fell, yet the space filled. Memory guided sinew. Desire shaped restraint.

Elena sobbed once, softly.

Bithia raised the bow.

The first stanza emerged like a promise kept—low, rounded, intimate. The sound settled immediately, touching the walls, the furniture, the hollow spaces grief had carved.

Elena's shoulders eased. Her head tipped gently to the side, breath slowing and smoothing. Rest found her the way a familiar melody finds its way home. A faint snore escaped her, almost apologetic, followed by a soft smile that lingered even as sleep claimed her fully.

The second stanza followed, richer, more assured. Anton closed his eyes, breath deepening though breath was no longer required. His expression softened into recognition. The bow traveled with confident weight, Bithia's wrist supple, her elbow yielding and gathering in seamless arc.

Cordelia resisted longer.

Her vigilance held, knuckles pale against the chair, eyes fixed and unblinking. Yet the music pressed gently at the places she guarded most fiercely. Her head dipped forward at last, resting against folded arms on the table. Sleep took her in fits and starts—brow furrowed, breath uneven—worry loosening its grip by degrees rather than surrender.

The third stanza resonated deeper still.

Bithia swayed now, movement born of alignment. The bow lengthened its path, drawing sound from the cello's depths. Anton moved with her, their expressions matching—brows raised, mouths softened, attention fixed inward. He rocked with the rhythm, guiding phrasing through proximity, through memory, through devotion.

Music braided them together.

The melody unfolded with patience and longing, filling the parlor with the gravity of a life shaped by listening. It offered rest where rest was needed.

The room responded—floorboards easing, fire settling into steady glow. Even the air seemed to settle slowly.

Bithia played on, lost within the sound, while Anton remained with her. Wrapped through her movement, her breath, her hands—as if the music held two souls at once.

And the cello, awake at last, answered each heart in the room.

Bithia swayed, body moving with the slow rapture of someone who had surrendered entirely. Her eyes were closed now, her expression serene, transported to someplace only music could reach. The shadows on the walls rippled as though keeping time, stretching and narrowing like dancers in low light.

Anton lifted his hand—just slightly.

The fire in the hearth flickered violently—once, twice—then fell still, cowed by the presence overtaking the room.

Elena sighed in her sleep, her smile deepening.

Cordelia's eyes fluttered, caught between worry and dream.

The tempo shifted. The melody deepened. For a heartbeat Cordelia felt it—truly felt it—press against her ribs. Urging her to quiet, to listen, to let go. Rest.

It was too much.

She surged forward, fueled by instinct rather than thought, and grabbed the bow from Bithia's hand.

Everything stopped.

The music dissolved mid-breath.

The air broke like a snapped string.

Anton vanished—released. His form collapsed back into the echo of the final note, as though he had never been separate from it at all.

Bithia slumped backward, gasping as though released from deep water. The cello hummed once more, then quieted.

Elena stirred, blinking as though waking from a perfect dream. Her smile remained.

Cordelia steadied herself, one hand braced against the table, breath coming a shade too fast.

"That," she said, voice uncharacteristically unsteady, "was not a séance."

"No," Elena murmured. Her fingers moved to her lips, as if surprised to find them there. "It was a gift."

Bithia raised her head slowly, eyes still luminous with the after-current of sound. "That has never happened before," she said, wonder threading her voice. "He...played through me."

Elena reached across the table and took her hand, her touch warm and grounding. "Anton was never ordinary," she said softly. "It seems fitting that he would find a way no one else ever has." A breath escaped her, lighter than any she had drawn since entering the house. "I didn't come seeking messages."

Cordelia's gaze sharpened, intent. "Then what *did* you come for?"

Elena looked down at the velvet sleeve, her thumb brushing the worn place where habit had lived. When she lifted her gaze again her eyes were clear—tender. No longer broken.

"You let his music breathe," she said. "You reminded me that it still lives. And somehow...so do I." A small, sincere smile touched her mouth. "My grief feels lighter now. Not gone. Just no longer carrying all the weight alone."

The sisters exchanged a glance.

Bithia's expression softened, filled with quiet compassion.

Cordelia's held steady—measured, thoughtful—caught between reverence and a dawning respect for what had passed through their care.

Elena gazed at La Dormiente with unshed tears.

"Anton's cello belong somewhere the music may still breathe," she whispered. "Somewhere quiet. Somewhere safe."

Elena traced the velvet sleeve one last time, her thumb brushing the worn place where Anton's hand had rested. Then she lifted her gaze to the sisters, eyes glistening but steady.

"I leave his music in your hands," she said softly. "Whatever lives within that bow...whatever remains in the cello...it trusts you more than it would anyone else. And so do I."

Cordelia inclined her head, solemn in a way she rarely allowed herself.

Bithia reached for Elena's hand, giving it a gentle squeeze.

"May peace follow you home, Mrs. Volterra," she murmured.

Elena nodded, gathering her cloak around her shoulders. She cast one last look at La Dormiente—its varnished surface glowing faintly in the candlelight—then stepped back from the table with quiet reverence.

The front door opened with a low, wintery groan.

Elena slipped into the night, the sound of her footsteps fading down the walkway like the final measures of a song.

When the latch clicked shut behind her, the house gathered the sound and held it. The floors stilled, the walls eased inward, and the weight of the cello seemed to sink gently into the structure. Claimed and sheltered, as if it had always belonged to the house's care.

Bithia gathered the cello case and the velvet-wrapped bow, the weight of both objects strangely gentle in her hands, and moved toward the staircase. The candle Cordelia carried cast a trembling halo around them, its flame wavering with each step they ascended. By the time they reached the landing the air had grown colder, thinner, touched with the stillness always associated with the attic.

Bithia pushed open the door.

The great room greeted them in silence. Dust motes drifted through the candlelight like pale ghosts, turning lazily as though roused from sleep. The shadows clung to the corners, waiting.

And there, in the closet beneath the slanted rafters, the trunk awaited—patient, solemn, as though it had known all along that another relic was coming home.

Cordelia leaned into the doorway, shawl pulled tight, expression unreadable in the half-light.

Bithia placed the bow gently inside the trunk, laying it among the other relics wrapped in time and sorrow. The flame guttered, then rose again.

She placed the cello—too large for the trunk—into the back of the closet beside it, propping it carefully against the wall where the shadows gathered thickest, as though appointed to the task.

The air drew close.

Cordelia spoke, her voice lowered, thoughtful rather than sharp.

"Do you suppose," she said, "that one day it will call to someone again?"

Bithia rested her hand on the trunk's edge, feeling the quiet weight of what laid inside.

"That is not for us to decide," she said. "We keep what is given. We listen. And when the time comes, we let it be claimed."

Cordelia considered this. Then, softer, as if addressing the room as much as her sister, she murmured,

"Very well. Then let it rest."

Bithia closed the trunk and pressed her palm to the lid.

The key turned.

The attic settled.

And deep within the closet La Dormiente stirred—a single, trembling vibration, so faint it might have gone unnoticed—before sinking back into stillness, as though drawing a long breath and surrendering to sleep.

A Birthday and a First Note

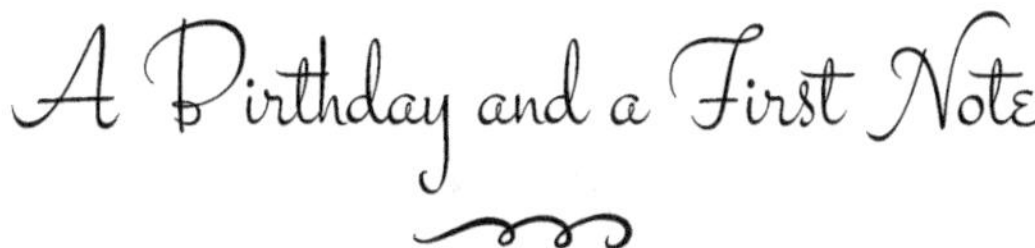

Sunlight found Nan long before she was ready to be awake.

A soft, honey-colored beam stretched across her face, warming the bridge of her nose and the tip of her cheek, gently coaxing her out of dreams. Without opening her eyes, she reached across the mattress for Mossy, finding—out of pure habit—the spot where his shoulder should have been.

Her fingers brushed only cool linens.

"Hm?" Nan's hand pattered across his pillow, confused for half a moment until her eyelids fluttered open. Mossy wasn't there. Instead, resting in the perfect hollow where his head had been, sat an envelope the color of midnight tides. Sealed with wax.

Nan smiled before she even fully woke. "Oh, Mossy..."

She reached for her glasses on the nightstand and knocked over *something*—either her water glass or the book of Browning poems Mossy had insisted she reread—but managed to snatch her spectacles before anything disastrous occurred. She perched them on her nose, broke the wax seal, and unfolded the thick paper.

His handwriting—curling, looping, proudly dramatic—met her like a kiss.

It was a sonnet, of course.

Her heart fluttered as she began to read.

My dearest Nan, at seventy you gleam,
A wisteria dawn in soft, unhurried bloom.
Where laughter ripens sweet as summer cream,
And love finds room to live in every room.

She paused, hand to her chest, as warmth unfurled inside her.

So may this day, my loveliest stanza yet,
Be crowned in joy no passing hour can steal.
For you, my Nan, make every year a duet—
A sweeter life no poet could conceal.

Nan pressed the note to her lips. After nearly five decades of marriage, Mossy still wrote her poems. And she still blushed like a girl discovering love for the first time.

"Well," she whispered to the empty room, "that man is going to make me cry before breakfast."

The room, apparently, disagreed about being empty.

A faint shimmer gathered near the wardrobe, the air thickening as though someone had stepped through a curtain Nan couldn't see. Cordelia appeared first, sharp as ever even in death, her expression already pinched with disapproval. Bithia followed more gently, her form coalescing beside the window, the morning light passing through her like breath through lace.

"Sentiment later," Cordelia said briskly. "If you wish to preserve what remains of your kitchen, I suggest you intervene."

Bithia inclined her head, sympathy softening her features. "The pixies are enthusiastic this morning," she added. "And your husband has given them...tasks."

Nan sighed, fond and resigned all at once. "It's my birthday," she said. "I was hoping for at least one quiet moment."

Cordelia sniffed. "Hope is admirable. Misplaced, but admirable."

Bithia smiled. "Go on," she urged. "We'll keep an eye on things up here."

Nan slipped from bed, tied the sash of her silk robe, slid her feet into soft slippers, and followed the noises drifting up from downstairs. Clattering, jingling, humming, and the unmistakable thwack of a wooden spoon hitting...something.

She paused halfway down the stairs, listening.

"Oh dear," she murmured. "That sounds structural."

Pixies.

Definitely the pixies.

Nan stepped into the kitchen—and stopped.

Chaos. Joyful, absurd chaos.

Flour footprints decorated the tile floor like pale bird tracks, looping and overlapping as if a flock had danced its way through breakfast. A tower of mixing bowls leaned at a reckless angle on the counter, defying gravity through either optimism or pixie insistence. In the largest saucepan a pixie stood ankle-deep in batter, gripping a wooden spoon nearly twice his height and stirring with the solemn concentration of someone performing sacred work.

That would be Neat—his moss-green coat carefully buttoned despite the mess, flour dusting his hair like snow.

"Circular motions," he muttered, nodding to himself. "Consistency matters."

Above him Thistle and Bramble swooped low near the ceiling beams, their wings humming as they chased one another in uneven loops. Thistle wore a muffin tin liner like a cape, zooming past the refrigerator with a dramatic flourish, while Bramble sneezed mid-flight and released a sparkling cloud of powdered sugar that drifted lazily toward the floor.

"Cover your mouth!" snapped Bitter from atop the spice rack, arms crossed, wings twitching irritably. "This is a kitchen, not a pollen festival."

Tansy perched on the windowsill, legs dangling, humming along to a tune only she seemed to hear. Meanwhile, Brash attempted—unsuccessfully—to carry three eggs at once, dropping one with a tragic gasp.

"Oh no," he said mournfully. "That one was my favorite."

And there—standing proudly atop the breadbox, chest puffed, curls wild as ever—was Bumbles.

Nan's heart lifted at the sight of him.

"Good morning, birthday maiden," Bumbles announced, bowing so deeply he nearly toppled forward. He recovered with dignity and beamed. "We have labored mightily in your honor."

He hopped down and presented her with a thimble-sized parcel wrapped in twine and a scrap of gingham.

Nan accepted it affectionately. "Why thank you, Bumbles."

Inside was a single button—blue glass, perfectly round, utterly unremarkable to anyone else.

"It came off Mossy's old cardigan," Bumbles said proudly. "We deemed it important."

"It's perfect," Nan said, meaning it.

Mossy—glorious, disheveled Mossy—stood in the midst of it all, flour-dusted apron askew, hair standing on end as he waved a spoon like a baton.

"Positions, everyone!" he called. "Breakfast waits for no one, least of all my beloved!"

The moment he saw Nan his entire face brightened, the chaos around him fading into irrelevance.

"My lady of the morning!" he declared, sweeping into a bow. "The sun itself pales beside you."

"Oh, Mossy." Nan couldn't help laughing. "What on earth have you done to my kitchen?"

Mossy pressed a hand to his heart, eyes bright with sincerity. "Improvised," he said gravely. "Like an evening of jazz and bourbon—structure abandoned in favor of feeling. And possibly butter."

He pivoted sharply, nearly colliding with Brash, then darted to the table with sudden reverence. From the midst of flour and crumbs he lifted something delicate and fragrant, cradling it as though it were a sacred relic.

He turned back to Nan, posture straightening, voice lowering into ceremony worthy of a coronation.

"For my beloved," he announced, "on the auspicious occasion of the culmination of her seventieth year."

A flower crown—woven from daffodils, daisies, and some glittery pixie-picked blossoms that definitely didn't grow in Florida.

He placed it on her head with reverence. "Your throne awaits, my love."

He pulled out her chair with a flourish. Nan sat, heart melting.

Pixies lined up on the counter like proud little sous-chefs.

Mossy presented her breakfast: a towering stack of pancakes dripping with whipped cream and strawberries, crowned by a single candle flickering bravely in the morning light.

He cleared his throat.

Then, with the solemnity of a man about to debut an opera no one had asked for, he began to sing.

"Happy birthday, my Nan of the morning," he intoned, drawing the words out.

"Happy birthday to *youuuuu*—

May your days be rhymed and your tea never bitter,

May your joys come buttered, and your troubles be little—"

The melody wandered off in search of itself.

A pixie—Bramble, Nan thought—leapt onto the counter and attempted to follow along, hitting the wrong notes enthusiastically. Thistle chimed in with a harmony that existed in an entirely different key. Bitter crossed his arms and muttered something about "artistic integrity" before joining in anyway.

Mossy pressed on, undeterred.

"Seventy years bright, and not done yet," he sang, voice cracking with feeling and absolutely no regard for pitch.

"My Nan, my love, my favorite stanza—

The poem I'd rewrite only to read again—"

Bumbles raised his tiny arms like a conductor, cueing the others.

"—again! again!" chorused the pixies, half a beat late and twice as loud.

Nan laughed so hard she had to steady herself in her chair.

"Enough, enough," she said, waving a hand as Mossy drew breath for what was clearly intended to be a final verse. And possibly an encore.

She leaned forward and blew out the candle. The flame winked out obediently, a curl of smoke rising between them.

Mossy bowed deeply, nearly knocking over the syrup.

"For you," he said simply.

And Nan, cheeks warm and eyes bright, thought there were worse ways to begin a birthday than being sung to—off-key, overlong, and entirely adored.

Coffee appeared at her elbow—poured by Mossy but carried by a pixie who tumbled midair the moment he handed her the mug.

"Oh!" Nan lunged and caught both mug and pixie. "Careful, Tansy."

The pixie sneezed again, coating her sleeve in sugar.

She didn't mind.

Just as she didn't mind that the kitchen looked like a midsummer storm had rolled through a bakery.

She was seventy today.

And her life—messy, magical, full of sweetness—felt impossibly rich.

When Mossy dropped to one knee beside her, dramatic as an opera tenor in the throes of death, she nearly spit her coffee laughing.

"Nan," he began, clasping her hand between his flour-dusted palms, "forgive me. Your birthday present—your grand, magnificent, heart-stirring surprise—is not yet ready for mortal eyes."

"Mossy, darling—"

"No, no." He tightened his grip, eyes bright with purpose. "You must wait. But when the moment comes, it will be... transcendent."

Pixies applauded with tiny hands.

Nan leaned down and kissed his forehead. "I trust you completely."

He softened at once, like butter left too near the stove. "Then my heart is at peace."

He rose, kissed her cheek, and with a dramatic sweep of his apron announced, "I must return to my secret endeavors! Adieu, my fair maid."

He departed the kitchen with great urgency—and a comet-tail of pixies scrambling after him.

Nan watched him go, her smile lingering even after the

doorway cleared. Nearly fifty years married and that man still found new ways to be entirely himself. Mossy loved through motion—through plans, through effort, through acts that required measuring tape and committees of pixies.

She loved that about him.

And still.

When the kitchen finally quieted, Nan sat back and let the morning settle into her bones. What she wanted, just then, was not a grand unveiling or a surprise wrapped in canvas and mystery. She wanted him at the table. His elbow brushing hers. His full attention, undivided and unhurried.

Seventy. The number hovered, unreal. Mossy's poem drifted back to her—wisteria dawns, laughter ripening, years unfolding gently. She held it close even as she felt the small, human wish beneath it.

He was proving his love the way he always had.

She simply wanted to sit in it for a while.

She closed her eyes, breathing in gratitude.

That was when she heard it.

Soft.

Full.

A single cello note—warm as candlelight—floating through the house.

Nan set her coffee aside and tilted her head, listening.

There it was again—that low, honey-warm hum. A single sustained note, full-bodied and resonant; the kind that wrapped itself around the bones rather than the ears.

"Could it be..." Nan rose halfway from her chair. "Mossy?"

She called his name down the hallway.

No reply.

She tried again. "Mossy? Are you playing something?"

Still nothing but the faint clatter of pixies reorganizing Mossy's abandoned mixing bowls.

Nan frowned. She crossed to the little radio perched on the kitchen counter and gave the dial a cautious twist.

Static whispered.

Then silence.

The note came again—clearer now. Deeper. As though someone plucked the heartstring of the house.

Nan's breath caught. "Is that…music?"

Another note followed.

This one bright, and unmistakably alive.

It wasn't recorded.

It wasn't Mossy.

It wasn't anything she could explain.

She was mystified. Enchanted.

The house had always held secrets, of course. Ghostly sisters, rambunctious pixies, rooms that liked to rearrange the furniture when bored. But this sound felt different.

Older.

Sleepy.

Lulling.

Nan made her way toward the staircase. Each step tingled beneath her slippers, as though the vibration of the unseen melody traveled up through the wood.

"That's absurd," she muttered, hand on the railing.

But the house seemed to urge her on.

She climbed slowly, breath lightening with each note drifting down to greet her. By the time she reached the attic landing, her heart was fluttering.

Her writing retreat sat bathed in morning sun—soft stripes of gold illuminating her oversized reading chair, the patchwork quilt folded neatly across its arm, her teapot still sitting from last night's work session.

Everything appeared ordinary.

But the sound continued. Thin at first, like someone

humming from another room. Then insistent—a gentle tug woven through the air.

Nan scanned the retreat.

The melody wasn't coming from the reading nook.

Or from her desk.

Or from the wind slipping through the cracked skylight.

It was coming from the closet tucked behind her writing desk.

The one that held the trunk in which Bithia's séance objects were encased.

Her pulse stumbled.

The house had a way of elevating ordinary moments to sacred.

Nan approached slowly, hand brushing the worn brass knob. She hesitated, breath catching on the edge of a familiar thrill.

Her fingers drifted, as they often did, to the chain around her neck.

The key—silver, warmed by years of contact with her skin, and subtly magical in the way of things that never announce themselves—rested against her collarbone. She had worn it since the day they'd found it, since the day the house had decided in its quiet way that they were meant to become a part of its story.

"Well," she murmured, thumb brushing the worn bow of the key, "if ever there was a day you were meant to unlock something..."

The key slid into the lock with familiar ease.

A soft click filled with recognition.

"All right," she whispered. "Show me."

The door opened.

Light from the attic window spilled inward, catching dust motes midair and turning them luminous, as though the room had been holding its breath until she arrived. They drifted lazily, unbothered, as if welcoming her rather than startled by intrusion.

This part of the house always felt different. More attentive. More alive.

Bithia's old séance trunk sat where it always had—broad-shouldered and iron-banded, draped in velvet that had once been plum and now lived somewhere between dusk and memory. Nan paused as she always did, acknowledging it with a glance and a quiet respect.

The trunk had a way of holding what the past left behind. Until the present was ready to receive it.

Objects had come and gone from it over the years—never loudly, never all at once. A music box that refused to stay silent. A monkey's paw that answered longing. Each item had arrived with its own gravity, had asked something of the house... And of the people living within it.

None of them had ever felt accidental.

Nan had come to understand that the closet—this narrow, slanted space tucked beneath the rafters—was something like the house's pulse point. Not the attic entirely, but this corner of it. Where memory lingered. Where emotion settled. Where the past was neither hidden nor forgotten, only *held*.

And then she saw it.

Behind the trunk—partially hidden, as though it had been waiting to be noticed rather than displayed—rested a large, elegant cello case. The leather was worn smooth along its edges, the marks of careful handling layered over decades. It had the quiet dignity of something loved and cherished.

Beside it lay a bow, wrapped in deep navy velvet.

The fabric was embroidered with delicate stitching—small, precise, and unmistakably human in its care. The kind of handiwork Nan had admired behind glass in museums, never expecting to encounter it like this. Intimate. Personal.

Her breath thinned to a ribbon.

"What on earth...?" she whispered. "That wasn't there before."

She knelt slowly, the movement deliberate. The faint hum she'd heard downstairs pulsed again—stronger now and unmistakable. It didn't echo through the room so much as *rise*, a subtle vibration that settled into her bones.

The house leaned in.

Nan reached out.

The velvet-wrapped bow thrummed beneath her fingers with the quiet insistence of something acknowledging touch. The sensation traveled up her arm like warmth through silk. Familiar, though she could not have said why.

Nan smiled, surprised by the ease of it. Music had always lived nearby—threaded through rooms, through years—but it had never asked anything of her before.

"Well," she murmured, more to herself than to the instrument. "Let's see where this leads."

She drew the bow free of its sleeve. The pernambuco wood gleamed softly in the attic light, the silver fittings dulled by years of use rather than neglect. Someone had loved this bow. Someone had shaped their hand around it until the balance became instinct rather than thought.

Nan lifted it.

The air beside her changed. The dust motes shifted. The light bent, altering its attention.

A figure hovered a half-step away, held in a gentle suspension that belonged to the ethereal plane. The room quietly accepted him. His shape was tall and composed, edges softened by light that passed through him without resistance, lingering just long enough to suggest form.

He wore a dark suit—charcoal, finely cut, close through the shoulders and waist. It was elegant without display, the kind of tailoring chosen by someone who understood restraint. The fabric caught the morning light and let it go again, not reflecting so much as suggesting movement. As though it had once followed the arc of a bow arm, the sway of a body deep in sound.

Nan felt calm amazement.

The presence regarded the cello with a focus so complete it felt intimate. One hand hovered near the instrument, not touching, never claiming. The other curved loosely at his side, fingers shaped as if they still knew tempo.

Nan's breath slowed to match the quiet between them.

She refrained from asking who he was.

She understood, without words, that he had come for the music.

His face was finely made—strong nose, thoughtful mouth, dark eyes alive with curiosity. His hair curled softly at the temples, exactly as it had in life, untouched by time.

Nan stared.

"Well," she said after a moment, because silence had never once improved her courage, "happy birthday to me."

The words settled easily in the attic air.

She glanced at him again—tall, dark, handsome in a way that felt intrinsic—and shook her head softly. "Seventy years on this earth, and this is what shows up in my closet. I suppose I should be flattered."

The figure's attention deepened. Not a smile, exactly—nothing so human. But a warmth moved through his expression, a recognition that met her humor without diminishing it. He inclined his head, just enough to acknowledge her not as an interruption but as a participant.

Nan felt absurdly pleased.

"Nannette Nettles," she continued, manners asserting themselves as they always did. "I bake. I host. I mind my business. And I appear to have stumbled on to something that matters to you."

She followed his gaze as it drifted gently and longingly toward the cello case.

He lifted one hand. Never touching. Never urging. Only offering the direction of attention, as though saying *there* without claiming ownership.

Nan nodded once, the decision already made.

"Well then," she murmured, warmth blooming in her chest, "let's not keep it waiting."

She knelt.

The latches yielded with a soft, satisfied click. When Nan lifted the lid, a familiar sweetness rose to meet her—old wood warmed by time, rosin lingering like memory, the quiet perfume of long devotion. The cello lay cradled within, its varnish glowing like amber caught mid-breath. The curves bore the language of years: a softened edge where a knee had rested, a faint hollow where a thumb had returned again and again, faithful as prayer.

A warmth gathered at her shoulder, the way a thought arrives fully formed, already shaped by feeling.

"La Dormiente."

The name came gently, settling into her mind as if it had always been waiting there.

Nan inhaled, slow and steady. Her pulse skipped. Not from fear but from surprise, the way one reacts when a door opens where no door had been before.

"Well," she murmured, because silence had never been her strongest suit, "that's new."

"She sleeps until she is needed," the voice continued—unspoken yet unmistakable. Musical. Measured. Italian in its cadence, even without sound. *"And when she wakes, she listens first."*

Nan didn't turn. She sensed rather than saw the presence beside her—attentive, composed, held in a luminous suspension.

"*My name is Anton,*" the voice offered, warm with courtesy rather than claim. "*Anton Volterra.*"

The name carried with it a fullness that made room in her chest, as though it had resolved something she hadn't known was unfinished.

"*This was my reason,*" he said, and the warmth deepened, aligning itself with her breath. "*Not halls or applause. This—*" and the intention moved toward the cello, radiant and patient, "*—this was my emotion made audible.*"

Nan's fingers tightened briefly on the edge of the case. She looked at the instrument again—not as an object now but as a held expression, waiting.

"Oh," she said softly. "You're beautiful."

The warmth at her shoulder gathered into something like gratitude.

Nan lifted the instrument.

She expected awkwardness. The heaviness of unfamiliar posture. The uncertainty of where to place herself in relation to something so serious.

Instead, the cello settled against her as though recognizing her shape.

Her knees found their distance. Her back straightened—comfortably, as if recalling a posture learned long ago and set aside. The instrument rested against her shoulder, warm and steady, and for the first time that morning she felt entirely located within her body.

Anton's hand hovered just above her left shoulder.

"Alright," Nan said softly. "Let's see what you have to say."

She raised the bow.

The first note emerged full and rounded, carrying warmth rather than volume. It moved through the attic and into the house below, easing into beams and corners with the assurance of something welcomed.

Nan inhaled with a rush.

Her arm moved again—and then she laughed.

The sound shifted beneath her bow. The string adjusted almost imperceptibly, sliding into truer pitch. The cello responded to the stroke with a faint, pleased hum, the wood vibrating in a way that felt more like a stretch than a sound.

"Well," Nan said softly, delighted, "aren't you clever."

"Again," Anton suggested—an invitation shaped by certainty. His presence aligned with her stance, attention flowing into the instrument. One luminous hand rested lightly along the cello's neck. The strings answered his touch.

Nan drew the bow once more. This time the pitch settled faster, the tone blooming clean and centered. A faint adjustment rippled through the body of the cello, like breath finding its proper place in the chest.

"Oh," she breathed. "You're tuning yourself."

"She remembers," Anton replied.

Nan shifted her grip instinctively—and felt a gentle correction, a suggestion carried through warmth rather than instruction. Her wrist softened. The angle of the bow changed by a whisper. The sound deepened.

"There you go," she murmured, absurdly proud.

The cello resonated in agreement.

As Nan moved from string to string, each one answered in turn—first tentative, then assured—settling into harmony as Anton guided her with the quiet precision of a life filled with long practice. Pressure eased where it needed easing. Weight found its balance. The bow no longer scraped or searched; it spoke.

Nan laughed again, low and delighted, the sound threading itself between notes.

"I've waited seventy years," she said, half to herself, half to the glowing presence beside her, "and today I get a cello that tunes itself and a spirit who knows exactly what he's doing."

Anton's warmth brightened, amusement shaping his silence.

Together, they played on—the attic listening, the house leaning in—as *La Dormiente* woke fully, stretching into her voice, pleased to be held once more by hands willing to learn.

"Well, this hardly seems fair," she whispered.

Anton's face brightened. He stepped closer, his form overlapping hers without obscuring it. His hand traced the arc of her bowing arm, never touching yet guiding with a precision born of thousands of hours in practice rooms and narrow stages.

They began a piece.

At first, it carried no title for her. Nothing she might have known how to hum before that moment. The melody moved forward with quiet patience, unfolding one phrase at a time, as though waiting to see what of herself she would offer.

She swayed—only slightly at first. The movement surprised her, then felt inevitable. Her body found the rhythm before her mind caught up, shoulders loosening, breath settling into the rise and fall of the notes. The bow ceased to feel like something she held. It belonged to her hand now, an extension rather than an instrument.

Her fingers pressed the strings with a confidence that bypassed thought.

The music remained gentle, almost neutral in its opening—clear, attentive. Unhurried. And then, without warning, something inside her opened.

Not images or scenes arranged in order.

Sensations.

Mossy's laugh surfaced first—not the sound of it, but the feeling it used to give her when they were young and reckless, when the future still felt vast and unclaimed. The note warmed and rounded, and Nan felt her mouth curve into a smile.

Another phrase opened.

Flour-dusted hands. Her first baking triumph. The thud of her heart as she realized she wanted this joy in her life—this pleasure—for herself. The bow pressed a fraction deeper. Pride moved through the sound, steady and earned.

The melody rose.

Wisteria at dawn. The way light pooled softly along the porch boards. The quiet satisfaction of a table set just right, of guests settling, of nourishment offered without fanfare. Her throat tightened just enough to register how deeply that care had mattered.

Her breath caught on the next note.

The sound opened into a sense of continuity, a feeling Nan had known in flashes but never named. She felt herself not as a single life but as part of a longer one. Mother. Grandmother. Great-grandmother. Each role layered gently upon the last, adding weight and meaning.

Women rose into the music then.

Presences. Her own mother's steady hands. Her grandmother's quiet competence. The women before them—some remembered, some only felt. Each life shaped by love, labor, endurance, and care. *Pearls*, she thought, *strung along the same silk thread.* Different sizes, different luster, each formed by time and pressure, all held together by something stronger than any one of them alone.

The bow slowed just enough to honor the thought.

She felt the children who had come after her, too—the small warm bodies she had held, the future unfolding outward beyond her sight. Continuation. The knowing that her hands had been part of the passing along. That her love had moved forward and would keep moving long after she was done carrying it herself.

Her eyes stung, gently. She blinked once and let the feeling remain.

The cello answered with a deeper warmth, as though it understood the shape of that knowing.

The music widened.

It gathered everything—effort, delight, loss, patience—and let it exist together without demand. The ache softened. The joy stayed.

Seventy.

The number entered the melody without resistance. It felt expansive. A wide, sunlit room with space enough to breathe.

Nan felt tears gather then. They slid free as she played, unnoticed until her vision blurred slightly and the sound grew richer for it.

Anton watched her with reverence, as though witnessing the purpose of his devotion fulfilled in a way he had never imagined could be shared. The cello's voice lived again, not through mastery but through a life that had learned how to listen.

Nan's eyes closed.

She played on.

The music held her years gently, allowing them to rest where they belonged.

When the final note resolved, it lingered just long enough to be acknowledged before easing back into quiet.

Nan lowered the bow.

Her hands trembled—from the afterglow of something deeply, unmistakably right.

She opened her eyes.

Anton hovered before her, his expression softened into something that looked very much like peace. He placed his hand over his heart and inclined his head once more—this time in thanks.

"Well," Nan said, voice thick but smiling, "that was a gift."

He reached out to the space between them, as if sealing an understanding that required no words. Then his form thinned, light passing through him more freely, his attention returning to the instrument that had carried his life forward.

Nan carefully set the cello back into its case.

Her birthday morning waited below. Flour and laughter. Mossy's earnest schemes. A house full of living hearts.

But for a moment longer she sat in the attic, bow resting across her knees, breathing in the quiet satisfaction of a life that had been fully, generously played.

Seventy, she thought.

What a beautiful number.

Schemes, Dreams, and a Disturbance in the Mulch

The side yard looked like a military encampment designed by a romantic poet and sabotaged by pixies.

White canvas tents billowed over the entire space, their ropes snapping lightly in the morning breeze. The clatter of tools echoed inside like distant thunder, metal striking metal in uneven rhythms. Pixies zipped overhead in erratic zigzags, ferrying nails, coils of twine, and—at one point—a single daffodil petal carried with solemn purpose, as though it had been requisitioned for morale.

Mossy stood at the center of it all and surveyed his domain.

In his mind, the tents were already gone.

In their place: water.

A pool curved gently into the shape of a heart, its edges smooth and pale beneath the sun. Lanterns glowed along the perimeter, reflected twice over in rippling blue. Fountains arced upward in soft, jubilant bursts, catching the light. And drifting lazily across the surface—absurd and perfect—were two enormous white swans, regal and ridiculous in equal measure.

Nan would laugh. He could hear it. That delighted, disbelieving laugh she saved for moments when something was both unnecessary and utterly right.

In another life—he was certain of it—he would have worn a laurel crown. He would have stood on newly claimed ground, soil still warm from effort, and declared it good. Claimed for devotion.

Veni, vidi, amavi, he thought, adapting Caesar to suit his needs.

The present returned in pieces.

He wore bright yellow rain galoshes because he didn't own, nor had he *ever* owned, work boots. A fluorescent safety vest hung off his shoulders like a disgruntled highlighter. The hard hat perched atop his silver hair was at least two sizes too big, tipping boldly to the left whenever he turned his head.

Still—regalia was regalia.

And this ground, chaotic as it looked now, would soon hold water and light and laughter. He only had to see it through.

The men with their tools were his legions. The pixies, unruly but loyal auxiliaries. And the ground beneath the tent—this patch of stubborn Florida earth—was being reshaped into something worthy of offering.

For Nan.

Mossy cleared his throat with professorial gravitas, straightening despite the tilt of his helmet.

Rufus stood at his side—long-limbed, bespectacled, and wearing a hard hat he had definitely pilfered from the back of someone's truck. His T-shirt loudly advertised a *Pickleball Invitational 2024*, and he adjusted his knee brace with the seriousness of a man preparing for Olympic trials.

Second-in-command, Mossy decided. Trusted advisor. The sort who might caution restraint while sharpening his sword.

"Rufus," Mossy intoned, lifting his chin, "bring forth the plans."

Rufus—long accustomed to being consulted before decisions of questionable wisdom—adjusted his glasses and reached for the blueprints. "You've been reading Roman history again, haven't you?"

Mossy smiled faintly, eyes still on the tented expanse.

"A man must know how to claim new ground," he said. "Especially when he intends to dedicate it to love."

Rufus bent with theatrical slowness, retrieving the rolled blueprints from a bucket of tools and slapping them into Mossy's hands with a flourish meant to imply competence.

Mossy unrolled the blueprints with great ceremony—

and instantly lost control of them.

Three pixies streaked overhead, shrieking with delight, playing tag with the enthusiasm of caffeinated toddlers who had just discovered the outdoors. Their wings churned the air into a mischievous breeze that caught the paper like a sail. The blueprints snapped upward, slapped Mossy squarely in the face, then launched themselves above his head, flapping wildly like a frantic seagull under siege.

"Merciful heavens!" Mossy cried, leaping after them.

He hopped.

He lunged.

At one point he executed a movement that could generously be described as interpretive dance.

"Hold the line!" shouted Brash, who wore a thimble on his head like a helmet and a scrap of foil strapped to his chest. "No retreat!"

"We are the vanguard!" yelled Thistle, swooping low with a paperclip sword clenched triumphantly in both hands.

Bramble, wrapped in a scrap of lace curtain like a toga, cackled as he tugged one corner of the plans. "The banner must fly!"

"Discipline!" Bumbles barked, attempting to sound authoritative while wearing a bottle cap shield and a necklace of mismatched buttons. "You'll tear the sacred parchment!"

"That is not parchment!" Bitter snapped, clinging to the opposite edge, wings buzzing irritably. "And you're wearing the butter lid again."

"Because it gleams," Bumbles replied.

The blueprints bucked and twisted between them, a battlefield of creases and corners.

Mossy spun beneath it all, arms flailing. He jumped once more, wheezed audibly, then—by sheer persistence rather than grace—caught hold of the paper's edge.

"Victory!" Brash cried, promptly letting go and saluting.

Mossy staggered back, clutching the plans to his chest. He flapped them several times in sharp, offended motions, as though scolding them back into obedience, then held them aloft like a dubious treasure wrested from chaos.

Rufus watched the entire spectacle without blinking.

When Mossy finally looked at him, breathless and triumphant, Rufus adjusted his glasses.

He tapped the paper with the pencil tucked behind his ear, adopting the grave expression of a man about to deliver a structural engineering verdict.

"Blueprints are supposed to be two-dimensional, Moss," he said. "Not aerodynamic."

Mossy straightened his hard hat, which had slid halfway over one eyebrow.

"They have spirit, Rufus. Passion. Momentum."

"They have a vendetta," Rufus replied dryly, pushing up his glasses. "Pretty sure you're holding it upside-down, Moss," he said, deadpan.

"It is right-side up," Mossy insisted, rotating the sheet. "Unless the pool is meant to be built in the neighbor's azaleas."

Rufus leaned in, considering. "Well… I've seen worse pickleball courts." He stroked his whiskers thoughtfully. "A daring choice."

Mossy sighed with the weight of a man carrying too many hopes and not enough construction experience. "We must persevere."

Before Rufus could offer an unhelpful rhyme, a fresh wave of chaos arrived.

Half the contractors trickled in late, wielding coffee and apologetic shrugs. The other half were already there but arguing about whether the rebar was supposed to go "northish" or "more to the heart's left ventricle." Someone had left the cement mixer running far too long.

Mossy tried to maintain composure—his Nan deserved grandeur, romance, perfection. But then the delivery truck backed into the tented yard and offloaded crates of the wrong tiles and a giant hippo statue carved from stone.

"No one ordered that," a contractor muttered.

But Mossy didn't hear him.

For Mossy the world had gone still.

Reverent.

Transfixed.

He placed a hand over his heart.

"Oh my stars," he breathed. "It's… magnificent."

And indeed, the hippo was a marvel—broad, generous curves carved with decadent care, as though the sculptor had channeled Rubens himself and declared, *Yes, but what if the classical nude were a hippopotamus?*

Mossy stepped closer, eyes shining.

"Look at the form, Rufus. The opulent sweep of the belly. The regal arch of the back. Those sumptuous folds—why, they rival Venus at her most triumphant. Rubens would have wept."

Rufus clasped his hands earnestly.

"I knew the hippo would please you."

"Nan loves hippos," Mossy declared, nearly emotional. "This is fate. Pure, unbridled fate."

The contractors stared at the statue with dawning horror, calculating the weight, the logistics, and the likelihood of workers' comp claims.

Pixies applauded like they were witnessing a coronation.

Mossy sighed dreamily.

"If this hippo were any more exquisite, it'd require a velvet rope and an art history lecture."

Mossy, standing tall in his galoshes, declared, "Gentlemen, we build love today!"

Mossy circled the hippo with the awe of a man witnessing divine intervention. For a fleeting, glorious moment he *saw it* —the entire project finished, a heart-shaped pool gleaming under fairy lights. Nan laughing, dazzled. The hippo presiding like a benevolent, curvaceous guardian of love.

Perfection.

Pure, sparkling perfection.

But then—

The vision shattered.

He blinked back to reality: mud, overturned crates, wrong tiles, late contractors, pixies arguing over a stolen wrench. The cement mixer groaned like a dying walrus.

Mossy's heart sank to his galoshes.

"Oh, Nan," he whispered. "You deserve better than this chaos."

He drew a slow breath, lifted his chin, and reached for steadiness where he always did—in the words of someone who understood perseverance as a form of love.

Do the work before you, he reminded himself. *Accept what is asked. Make it worthy.*

Rufus, reading his face without comment, gave his shoulder a firm, grounding pat.

"Still fixable," he said softly.

Mossy nodded once.

Yes. Still fixable.

The hippo gazed on, serene.

And Mossy prayed he hadn't bitten off more metaphor than he could chew.

A sudden temperature drop slipped through the tent, lifting the fine hairs on Mossy's arms. The canvas walls fluttered—not with wind but with displeasure.

Rufus glanced around. "Did someone open a door?"

"No," Mossy murmured, already bracing.

A soft shimmer gathered beside the hippo statue, the air bending inward like a curtain drawing itself.

Cordelia materialized.

Pale as frost, elegant as ever, her Victorian silhouette sharpened by an expression that could curdle cream. Only Mossy and Rufus could see her; the contractors remained blissfully unaware. One walked straight through the edge of her skirt and shivered violently without knowing why.

"Mossy," she snapped, voice ringing with century-old indignation, "must you desecrate my grounds with these infernal machines?"

A contractor nearby startled, dropping his trowel.

Mossy lowered his head and pinched the bridge of his nose. "Forgive me, dear Cordelia. It's a birthday surprise for Nan."

Cordelia crossed her arms, forming an angle of aristocratic disapproval.

"Well... be rid of the noise quickly. A ghost cannot haunt effectively with all this clatter."

Rufus—who heard only Mossy's side of the conversation but guessed as to what was vexing her—added helpfully, "We'll be quick as crumpets, your ladyship."

Cordelia's irritation pressed into Mossy's ribs, amplifying the ache already there. Then her posture wavered.

Just a flicker. But enough to hint that beneath her disapproval lived the faintest echo of interest.

"You love your lady," she said, voice gentler than he expected. "As long as that remains true... the rest is tolerable."

Mossy blinked. "That is the highest praise you've ever given me."

With a scowl on her face, Cordelia dissolved into a cold ripple of air.

Mossy straightened his vest. Adjusted his too-big hard hat. Placed a hand on the hippo's rounded flank for luck.

"I will make this present perfect," he vowed.

Rufus saluted with the pencil.

The pixies cheered like unpaid interns.

And the hippo statue gazed at him serenely... as though blessing the endeavor with ancient, hippo-shaped wisdom.

The cello was not heavy exactly, but it was substantial—long-limbed and elegant, its polished wood catching the light as though pleased to be back out in the open. Nan hugged it close, one arm wrapped around the curved body, one hand gripping the neck while the bow rested precariously in her free hand.

She negotiated the stairs sideways, heels placed carefully on each polished tread, the wrap dress she'd chosen for her birthday morning swishing softly around her calves. The pearls at her throat caught the light as she moved. Overhead, the chandelier winked encouragement, its crystals chiming faintly with each step as though offering moral support.

"Well," Nan muttered, pausing on the landing to readjust her grip and rescue the bow from sliding down her wrist, "this is certainly a birthday surprise I didn't see coming."

She glanced behind her then, half-expecting to find the tall, attentive presence from the attic lingering in the hallway. The space remained empty. No shimmer. No hovering courtesy. Just the familiar hush of the house settling around her.

All right, she thought calmly. *You'll come when you're ready.*

She continued on, marveling at the instrument—the graceful sweep of its curves, the deep, honeyed sheen of the varnish. A beautiful thing. A serious thing. And hers, at least for the moment. Found tucked away in her own attic on the very morning she turned seventy, no less. Life, it seemed, still held a fondness for timing.

Nan had always loved music. Admired it. Revered it from a respectful distance. She'd married a poet, after all. Mossy's words were music, in their own way—lyrical, meandering, occasionally impractical. Playing, however, she'd always assumed belonged to other people. People who started young. People with lessons and posture and confidence.

Not women who served high tea and negotiated calmly with Victorian ghosts. Who gently redirected high-spirited pixies and yet still found themselves carefully inching a cello down polished wooden stairs, whispering encouragement to themselves and the bow they were determined not to drop.

She reached the bottom at last and exhaled, victorious.

"There," she told the cello softly. "See? We manage just fine."

She paused, listening. Not with her ears exactly, but with the quiet awareness that had taken up residence somewhere behind her ribs.

Nothing stirred.

Nan smiled anyway, adjusted her grip, and carried on.

The parlor was just as she'd left it earlier that morning. Sunlight slanted through lace curtains. The piano sat quietly in the corner like a dignified relative who had already had their morning tea and read the headlines. The scent of fresh polish mingled with lemon and something floral from the garden.

From the kitchen came the clatter of pans and the unmistakable sound of Mabel singing.

Nan didn't recognize the song—something lilting and half-invented, with lyrics that wandered freely and a tune that changed keys whenever it pleased. Mabel's voice rose and fell as she worked, punctuated by the *thunk* of drawers and the clink of fine china. There was comfort in it. Habit. The sound of someone filling space so it wouldn't echo.

Good, Nan thought. *I have a moment.*

She set the cello gently near the window, its polished curves catching the morning light, and stood there for a breath longer than necessary, hands still resting against the warm surface. The memory of earlier lingered in her chest. As sensation. As fullness. As the unmistakable pull of something that had not finished with her yet.

She had played that morning.

And the emotion it had sparked within her still lingered.

Nan exhaled, a small, amused sound leaving her. "Well," she said to no one in particular, "let's see if it has more to say."

The simple truth was that the cello had opened something, and she wished—quite dearly—to step back inside it.

She lifted the instrument again, already smiling.

She turned and lowered herself into the black lacquer chair, its surface gleaming softly, the mother-of-pearl inlay winking up at her lovingly. The chair made her smile every time she passed it. It had been one of those finds—beautiful, impractical, and utterly irresistible. Mossy had called it dramatic. Nan preferred *characterful.*

Now, it felt... appointed.

"Well," she intoned softly, settling in, "if one were ever going to declare a throne for music..."

She adjusted the cello and it settled against her shoulder as though it had been waiting for exactly this invitation. Her knees found their proper distance without thought. Her posture aligned comfortably. Naturally, like stepping into a familiar routine.

The air shifted.

Nan didn't look around just yet. She lifted the bow first, aware—gently, unmistakably—that she was no longer alone.

When she finally glanced to her side, he was there.

Anton, composed and attentive, his form held in a soft glow. He looked at home with the space.

His gaze moved toward the kitchen doorway as Mabel's voice rang out.

Nan followed his attention.

"Oh," she breathed, understanding blooming without instruction.

He inclined his head, the dark curls of his hair covering his eye.

Nan drew the bow across the strings. The first note bloomed with warmth. Roundness. Then the sound settled like a shawl drawn around the parlor's shoulders.

The melody curved gently, familiarly. It carried the shape of old hills and steady footsteps. A tune meant to be followed rather than memorized. Nan felt it settle into her bones before it reached her ears.

From the kitchen, Mabel's singing faltered.

Nan played on.

The bow guided itself into a slower rhythm, the music rocking rather than driving forward. A lullaby, though no cradle waited for it. A song meant for someone who carried more than they ever set down.

Anton moved with the phrasing, aligning rather than directing. His presence gathered close to the sound, shaping the narrow, intimate space where bow met string. When Nan's pressure grew too firm the tone rounded, easing her hand. When the line wavered the melody found its footing again, steady as breath.

Nan laughed softly under her breath, surprised by her own delight.

As the notes unfurled, images began to surface. Impressions layered through the sound. Petals opening in sequence. Stems bending toward light. A garden arranged for meaning. White blossoms for remembrance. Yellow for quiet joy. Blue for patience. Purple for devotion.

The knowledge arrived whole.

Of course, Nan thought, warmth spreading behind her ribs. *That's how Mabel experiences the world.*

From the kitchen drifted the faintest hum—Mabel's voice, unsteady now, the tune loosening its edges as the music reached her. Nan felt the response ripple through the house like a breeze passing through tall grass. The melody shifted just slightly, leaning into gentler intervals, resting longer on certain notes as though offering comfort.

Above her head a pixie drifted lazily through the air, wings slowing mid-beat before it settled atop the curtain rod. Its eyes closed with a small, satisfied sigh, hands folding neatly in its lap as if lulled by something deeply familiar.

Nan played on, understanding settling quietly into her hands.

The house was listening, too.

Time loosened.

Nan swayed with the music, shoulders easing, breath finding its own cadence. The melody carried something tender now—rest offered without demand. She thought briefly of hands folded at a kitchen table. Of someone who worked early and late, who sang to fill quiet spaces.

In the kitchen, a pan slipped from Mabel's grasp and clattered softly to the floor.

Nan continued.

The music wrapped itself around the house, threading through doorways and corners, settling where it was needed. The clock's ticking thinned. The ocean breeze at the window hushed.

Then—dimly—another sound intruded.

Bright. Mechanical.

Insistent.

Nan frowned, the melody bending slightly around the interruption before releasing it.

The front doorbell.

She stopped playing, the final note stretching and thinning until it slipped neatly back into silence.

Anton remained for a breath longer, his attention lingering toward the kitchen. Then the space eased. The light reclaimed itself.

Nan sat very still.

"Well," she said softly, heart full and steady, "that was... all-encompassing."

She set the cello aside with care, smoothing her dress as she rose.

The doorbell rang again.

"Just a moment, I'm coming!" she called, already moving, carrying with her the quiet certainty that the music had known exactly what it was doing.

As she crossed the parlor Mabel shuffled in from the kitchen, yawning broadly and rubbing one eye.

"Nan," Mabel said, voice thick with sleep, "I don't know what came over me. One minute I was singing, and the next —" She gestured vaguely toward the hallway. "Gone."

Nan frowned. "You fell asleep?"

"Like a cat in a sunbeam," Mabel confirmed. "Strangest thing."

Nan glanced back at the cello, then quickly away again.

"Well," Nan said lightly, adjusting the shawl at her shoulders, "you've been up since dawn. Anyone would doze."

Mabel nodded, blinking as though surfacing from a pleasant dream. "Must be the weather," she said thoughtfully.

"That, or the fact that I cleaned up Mossy's birthday breakfast while you were readying yourself for the day."

Nan winced. "Oh, Mabel—I meant to—"

Mabel waved a hand decisively. "No, I won't hear it. You're the birthday girl today." She peered around the parlor, hands on her hips. "Besides, it was a simple enough thing. Crumbs, plates, nothing too crazy."

Nan felt warmth rush to her face. "I'm perfectly capable of washing a few dishes."

"Not today," Mabel said firmly. "Not one finger. Not a single helpful impulse. You turn seventy once, Nanette, and when you do the rest of us see to things." She narrowed her eyes kindly. "That includes not sneaking back into the kitchen to 'just straighten up'."

Nan laughed, caught. "I don't sneak."

Mabel arched a brow.

Nan conceded the point with a smile.

Mabel glanced toward the window then back at Nan. "Now," she said briskly, "if you'll excuse me, I believe it's time for tea—or at least the suggestion of it. And if anyone asks, you are to be sitting. Preferably with music nearby."

She paused, her gaze drifting across the parlor again. "Are the pixies napping?"

Nan followed her gaze, smiling to herself as she took in the room—quiet, settled. Gently at rest.

"Yes," she said softly. "I think they are."

One pixie was curled in the curtain folds. Another had settled in the bowl of decorative stones by the fireplace, snoring faintly. A third lay sprawled across the piano bench, arms flung wide in dramatic exhaustion.

Nan stared for a moment longer than strictly necessary.

"Hm," she said at last. "Busy morning."

The doorbell rang a third time, brighter now and more insistent.

Nan straightened. "Guests," she said with a smile, already shifting into hostess mode. "Show time."

She headed for the door, the cello resting quietly behind her—silent, patient, as though it had done exactly what it came to do.

For now.

Brisk and cheerful, Nan shook off the lingering warmth of the music as she crossed the parlor.

"Coming!" she called again, already smiling.

When Nan opened the door, she was greeted by movement before words.

Maren Clay stepped forward at once, brushing imaginary crumbs from the front of Walter's tweed vest with brisk, affectionate swipes. "Honestly, Walter, you had that disgusting breakfast sandwich in the car. You are wearing half of it. How do you manage that?"

Walter glanced down at his vest, unfazed. "I don't see anything," he said mildly.

"That's because you never do," Maren replied, already smiling at Nan. "Hello! You must be Nan Nettles."

Walter adjusted the folded newspaper tucked beneath his arm and inclined his head politely. He stood tall, back straight. Despite the Florida warmth his button-down was crisply pressed, his vest neatly fastened, and his shoes polished to a quiet shine. He looked like a man who had spent a lifetime following instructions—and had learned somewhere along the way that doing so made things easier for everyone.

"I'm Maren Clay," she continued, already extending her hand before Nan had time to respond. Her grip was warm and earnest, her smile bright enough to suggest she rarely waited for permission to like people. "And this is my husband Walter."

She smoothed the lapel of his jacket, which did not appear to need smoothing.

"We have a reservation—oh! I hope we're not early. Or late." She laughed, the sound light and musical as she shifted her large canvas tote higher on her shoulder. The rose-colored dress she wore fluttered gently in the breeze, cheerful and soft, its skirt swaying with every animated movement. Pearl earrings winked at Nan as Maren spoke. "We came down from Jacksonville this morning, which was quite the drive because Walter insists on taking the scenic route even when the scenery is mostly billboards."

Walter opened his mouth. Closed it. Adjusted the folded newspaper beneath his arm and looked past Nan toward the hallway with polite interest, as though the architecture might intervene on his behalf.

"We found you on the internet," Maren went on, undeterred, already leaning forward conspiratorially. "There was this story—about a monkey? Or a paw?" She glanced at Walter, eyebrows rising expectantly. "Walter, was it a monkey?"

"A paw," Walter supplied dutifully.

"Yes! A paw." Maren clapped her hands once, delighted. "Very unsettling. But also comforting? Which is not a sentence I ever thought I'd say." She laughed again, reaching into her tote as if she might produce the article itself at any moment. Nan caught a glimpse of a small notebook inside, its corners softened with use. "Anyway, we thought—well, this feels like the sort of place where one might..." She paused, searching for the word, then smiled softly. "...rest."

Nan smiled back, already fond.

"You've come to the right place," she said warmly. "Please come in."

Maren beamed and stepped inside without hesitation. Walter followed, pausing just long enough to wipe his shoes carefully on the mat before crossing the threshold.

Just then, a tremendous *clang* echoed from the side yard,

followed by a rumble, a shouted apology, and Mossy's unmistakable voice rising in poetic distress.

"That is not the angle we discussed!" he called out, sounding both wounded and philosophical. "One cannot rush symmetry! This is not a casserole!"

Nan closed her eyes briefly and smiled.

"I do apologize for the noise," she said, lowering her voice conspiratorially. "My husband is... in the midst of a birthday surprise."

As if summoned by the word *birthday* another metallic thud rang out, followed by Mossy again:

"No one touch the hippopotamus!" Mossy called. "Her heart is too tender, her gaze far too dear for careless hands."

Maren's eyes widened with delighted curiosity. She glanced toward the canvas walls visible through the window, then back at Nan.

"Well," she said, cheerful awe creeping into her voice, "it must be quite the surprise if it requires a house-sized tent and heavy machinery."

Nan laughed. "My husband's very thorough."

Walter nodded once, solemnly, as though this explained everything.

"Oh, Walter, look at this room!" Maren exclaimed. "The light! And those curtains—I told you this place would be charming!"

Walter nodded, glancing around with quiet approval. "Solid floors," he said. "Good bones."

Nan laughed. "Tea and scones?" she offered. "You look like you've earned them."

Maren clasped her hands. "Oh, yes please. We've been up since dawn. Walter insisted on stopping twice for coffee."

"Three times," Walter corrected mildly.

Nan led them to the seating area, where Maren settled eagerly, leaning forward. Walter sat back more carefully, unfolding his newspaper before setting it aside—an unconscious habit, Nan noted, but a telling one.

A clatter of china announced itself from the kitchen before Nan could say another word.

"Perfect timing," Nan said, turning just as Mabel appeared in the doorway.

Mabel balanced a tray with practiced ease—teapot steaming, two plates of scones nestled beside small dishes of jam and clotted cream. She wore her gardening apron over a pair of wide-leg trousers printed with riotous florals, the colors clashing cheerfully in a way that somehow worked on her. Her short auburn hair curled softly around her face, and her smile was the kind that made rooms feel brighter simply by existing in them.

"Mabel," Nan said fondly, "may I introduce Walter and Maren Clay. They've just arrived."

Mabel beamed at them. "Oh! You're the Jacksonville couple. We've been expecting you."

Walter blinked. Maren laughed immediately, delighted.

"And this," Nan added, with unmistakable warmth, "is Mabel. My dearest friend. If you admire the flowers anywhere in this house—or outside of it—those are her doing."

Mabel waved a dismissive hand, already setting cups onto the low table. "Oh, I just listen. The garden tells you what it wants if you're polite about it."

Nan smiled. "All the bouquets you see—every arrangement—are hers."

"And grown right here?" Maren asked, leaning forward to peer more closely at the arrangement on the piano.

"Mostly," Mabel said. "Though I do get a little help."

She lowered her voice conspiratorially. "The cats supervise. The pixies rearrange things when I'm not looking."

Walter's mouth twitched. Maren laughed again, assuming—quite reasonably—that this was a joke.

"Well," Maren said brightly, accepting her teacup, "they're beautiful."

"Credit where it's due," Mabel said solemnly. "The roses insisted on that vase. I wanted something taller."

Nan caught the slightest flicker of movement near the mantel—something small and winged ducking behind a picture frame—but said nothing.

Tea was poured. Scones were passed. The parlor settled into that gentle, welcoming hush it always found when guests were properly installed.

And behind Nan, unnoticed, the cello rested in the corner —quiet, patient, waiting.

They talked easily as they ate.

Maren filled the space with gentle chatter—about the drive down, the beaches they'd passed, how long it had been since they'd taken a proper trip together. She spoke with the hopeful brightness of someone determined to *make something special happen*.

"We've been married forty-five years," she said. "And we thought—well—maybe it was time to remember how to be newlyweds again."

Walter nodded, reaching for another scone. "She planned the whole thing."

"I made a list," Maren said proudly, pulling out the notebook. "'Things We're Doing Together'. Sunrise walks. Holding hands. Talking without the television on."

Walter glanced at Nan, his expression softening just a fraction. "I'm trying," he said softly.

Nan felt her heart warm.

"I think that's a lovely reason to travel," she said.

As Maren set her teacup down her gaze drifted across the room, and landed on the cello resting near the window.

"Oh," she said, eyes lighting up. "What a beautiful instrument."

Nan followed her gaze. "That? Oh—I just found it in the attic this morning."

Maren leaned closer. "Do you play?"

Nan laughed, a little self-conscious. "I'm not sure that's the right word. I'm... experimenting."

Walter chuckled softly. "Brave of you."

"Well," Nan said with a smile, "it's my birthday. Seemed like a good day to try something new. Now that I've started, I can't seem to stop."

Maren clapped her hands once, thrilled. "You absolutely must play for us."

Nan felt warmth bloom in her cheeks. "Oh, I don't know about must," she said, though her smile held.

"Yes, play," Mabel said, already settling herself onto the piano bench with her teacup. "It feels like the kind of afternoon that wants music."

Nan hesitated just long enough to feel the familiar pull. The cello waited for her, calm and certain, as though the decision had already been made and she was simply catching up to it.

She rose, smoothed her dress, and lifted the bow.

"Well," she said lightly, "just a little, then."

As she positioned the cello, the room shifted.

Anton appeared at her side, borne into view as naturally as breath following a held note. He observed. His gaze moved first to the cello, then outward—toward the people gathered, curious.

Nan drew in a breath and began.

The first note slid into the parlor with warmth and clarity, settling into the space as though it had been expected. It vibrated through Nan's chest, down her arms, into the soles of her feet. Her shoulders loosened. Her spine found ease. She rocked gently as she played, motion guided by phrasing.

Anton tilted his head, listening.

The melody unfolded in layers. For Walter, it softened into something spacious and unhurried—long lines, steady cadence. The musical equivalent of an open road with no schedule attached. His shoulders sank back, his breath deepened, and he sighed—a contented, unguarded sound. The newspaper slid from his lap and folded itself at his feet. A moment later, his mouth fell open just slightly.

Maren reacted differently.

Nan saw it even as she played.

The music quickened around her—not faster, but brighter, nimble as a hummingbird. Notes flickered and darted, playful but insistent, circling themes without landing on them right away. Maren's smile widened. She tapped her fingers against her knee once… twice… then stilled.

Her eyelids fluttered.

"No, no—write that down," she murmured suddenly, eyes closed. "We can't forget the candles. And the bakery. And—oh, we're late."

Walter made a soft snorting sound and shifted, one hand drifting instinctively to cover hers.

Maren leaned into him, still murmuring. "Just one more thing… one more…"

Then her breath evened, the tension leaving her frame as though she'd finally been allowed to stop running.

Anton watched her closely. Recognition passed over his features. He glanced at Nan, just briefly.

Yes, his expression seemed to say. *That.*

Mabel, meanwhile, had slipped sideways on the piano bench, forehead resting against the fallboard, fingers still curled protectively around her teacup. A faint hum escaped her—half a tune, half a sigh—as though the music had followed her inward and found a garden there.

Above them, pixies drifted downward like bits of pollen caught in afternoon air. Tansy nestled into the daffodil centerpiece, sighing happily. Bitter wedged himself into the curve of a lampshade. Bramble attempted to stay upright midair, failed, and landed gently on the rug. "Worth it," he mumbled, already asleep.

Nan faltered.

Just for a breath.

Oh no, she thought, heat rushing up her neck. *I've done it again.*

Anton's attention returned to her at once. His presence aligned with hers, steadying the phrasing, reminding her to trust the sound.

She played on to the sleeping room.

The cello responded, shaping itself around the needs of the ones in need of rest.

When the final note resolved, it lingered long enough to be felt—then released itself into the quiet.

Nan lowered the bow.

The parlor breathed.

Walter drooled. Just a little.

Maren snorted softly and whispered, "I'll get to it tomorrow."

Nan covered her mouth with her hand to keep from laughing aloud.

"Well," she said softly, setting the bow aside, "that's one way to host an afternoon."

She glanced at Anton.

He hovered near the window now, attention resting on the sleepers with the calm satisfaction of a man reviewing a finished score. The cello answered his regard with a faint, lingering vibration.

Nan rose carefully, easing the instrument to its side where it could rest against the wall.

"Must be the drive," she decided kindly. "Or the tea. Or the ocean air."

From the hallway came the faintest disturbance. A tightening of the air, like fabric being drawn smooth.

Nan turned her head just in time to see Bithia and Cordelia hovering at the threshold.

Bithia's gaze moved first—to the sleeping guests, the pixies curled in improbable places, the stilled clock. Then to the cello. And finally—without surprise or hesitation—to Anton.

Her expression softened with recognition.

Cordelia, arms folded, took longer. Her eyes narrowed slightly as she took in the scene: the sprawled limbs, the unfinished gestures, the peculiar, deliberate stillness. When her gaze landed on Anton her mouth pressed into a thin, thoughtful line.

"Well," Cordelia said at last, voice pitched low, "that explains it."

Nan blinked. "Explains what?"

Her eyes returned to the cello. "That instrument is doing more than entertaining."

Anton inclined his head to them both, a courtesy returned to its proper place.

Bithia met the gesture with a small nod of her own. "Music has always been persuasive," she said. "But this..." Her gaze drifted back to the sleepers. "This has intention."

Cordelia's eyes sharpened. "Selective," she agreed. "Purposeful."

Nan felt the words settle somewhere beneath her ribs. She hadn't fallen asleep while playing—not once. Instead, she'd slipped into a clarity so complete it felt like standing inside beauty itself. A rest that didn't dull her but widened her. As though the years she carried had been set down, examined with affection, and handed back lighter.

She wanted—achingly—to play again.

Not for anyone. Not for the room.

Just for that feeling.

Bithia turned then, her expression gentle and certain. "The attic doesn't keep relics," she said. "It keeps answers. What it releases is never random. It offers what is needed, when and to whom it is needed."

Her eyes warmed as they met Nan's. "Today, it chose you."

Cordelia sniffed, though there was no real heat in it. "It seems the house has a flair for the dramatic." She glanced pointedly at the cello. "A rather elaborate birthday present."

Nan laughed under her breath, smoothing her skirt. "I was expecting a quiet morning and perhaps a scone."

Cordelia scoffed, the sound crisp and unmistakable. "Quiet?" She arched a brow. "In this house? With Mossy Nettles roaming about and Rufus emboldened by even the smallest hint of a project?" Her gaze flicked toward the parlor, where sleepers breathed in peaceful disarray. "You set your expectations dangerously high."

Bithia's smile softened, something knowing passing through her eyes. "You were seeking quiet," she said to Nan. "And the house heard you."

Nan glanced toward the cello. "I believe it gives rest in many forms."

Cordelia sniffed again, though her tone lacked its usual sharpness. "A unique birthday offering."

Anton moved then, fully into the moment. His voice arrived the way music does in memory: already known, already trusted.

"Nanette," he said.

Her name settled into her like a hand finding its place.

"You believe rest means the world growing quiet," he continued gently. "But quiet is only one language."

He looked not at the sleepers but through them, as if listening for what lay beneath their breath.

"Rest is when nothing inside you is straining to be elsewhere. When effort releases its grip. When the soul is no longer rushing ahead of the body… or dragging behind it."

The words did not press. They *tuned.*

"This house does not still people," Anton said softly. "It listens. And it answers what it hears."

Nan's throat tightened with recognition.

"You have given many others permission to rest," he went on, his gaze returning to her at last. "Today, the music has done the same for you."

The room seemed to draw inward, holding the truth of it the way a string holds tension—ready, balanced, alive.

Nan swallowed, her eyes bright.

He had spoken directly to the ache she'd learned to carry without complaint.

Nan understood then that rest was not something the world granted, nor a pause from living.

It was a choice made only once one loved oneself enough to stop pushing through.

"Well," she said instead, because she was still Nan, still the hostess, still grounded in the comforts of the living world, "fresh tea will be ready when they wake."

Bithia smiled.

Cordelia allowed herself the barest curve of approval.

And behind them all, the cello rested—awake, patient, and listening.

The concrete slid from the truck in a thick, unstoppable ribbon; gray and heavy and full of promise. The rumble of the mixer vibrated through the ground like a drumbeat, steady and relentless. Steam rose faintly where warm slurry met cool morning air.

Mossy stood at the edge of the pit with his arms raised.

"Easy now," he called, palms sweeping outward in a gesture that suggested both restraint and destiny. "Slow and steady. As the Romans would have wanted."

No one asked which Romans. No one needed to.

He paced the perimeter of the excavation, boots sinking slightly into damp soil, fluorescent vest flaring like a battle standard. His hard hat had slipped crooked again but he ignored it. A general didn't fuss with his helmet while history was being made.

Below him, the foundation curved into its shape—unmistakable, intentional. A heart pressed into the earth. The edges were clean. The lines true. Even unfinished, it carried meaning.

Nan's heart, made visible.

Mossy's chest tightened as he watched the concrete settle.

He could already see it finished. Lanterns glowing at dusk. Water catching the light. Swan floaties drifting in lazy circles while pixies argued about whose turn it was to ride the tallest one. Nan's laugh ringing out, delighted and surprised and exactly the sound he loved most in the world.

"We are close," he murmured, half to himself and half to the universe. "Very close."

A shout rang out.

"Uh—sir?"

Mossy turned.

The sound that followed was wrong. Too sharp. Too sudden. A metallic crack, followed by a hiss that escalated into a roar.

Water exploded upward.

A geyser shot straight out of the ground, arcing wildly before crashing down into the fresh concrete. Gray slurry splattered across the pit, the planks, the workers—and Mossy's boots.

Cold water soaked instantly through his socks.

For one suspended moment, no one moved.

Then everything happened at once.

"Sprinkler line!" someone yelled.

The water surged harder, churning the surface of the concrete into ripples. The carefully smoothed edges began to sag, the heart's graceful curve blurring as slurry loosened and slid.

"No," Mossy breathed.

The word left him quietly. Like a prayer spoken too late.

Pixies shrieked with delight.

They darted straight into the spray, wings flashing, hair plastered to their faces. One skidded across a wet plank on his stomach, laughing wildly. Another flung her arms wide and spun beneath the falling water like it was midsummer rain.

"Festival!" Brash cried.

"Battle rain!" Bitter shouted.

Bumbles whooped, already climbing a stack of lumber to leap dramatically into the puddling chaos.

"Stop—no—please don't—" Mossy began, then faltered.

The concrete shifted again.

The heart sagged.

The edges softened. The symmetry wavered.

Mossy felt it land in his chest with a dull, awful weight.

He stood very still as water continued to pour; boots filling, vest darkening. The vision he'd been holding—so bright, so certain—fractured. Lanterns dimmed. Swans drifted away. Nan's laugh faded, replaced by the sharp ache of disappointment he could already imagine too clearly.

"I was supposed to get this right," he said softly.

The words barely carried over the roar of water and machinery, but they mattered all the same.

Rufus moved to his side.

He didn't speak at first. He just stood there, solid and present, one hand resting lightly against Mossy's arm. A quiet anchor amid the chaos.

"It's not over," Rufus said at last, calm as a man discussing weather. "Sprinklers can be shut off. Concrete can be... encouraged."

Mossy swallowed.

He stared down at the heart-shaped hollow, at the place where devotion had been meant to set into something permanent. He had wanted this to be perfect. Not grand for the sake of it but perfect because Nan deserved care shaped into something you could see and touch.

"I wanted to give her joy," he said. "Something she didn't know she needed."

Rufus nodded. "You still can."

Another surge of water splashed across the pit. Pixies shrieked again, delighted beyond reason.

Mossy closed his eyes for a brief, unguarded second.

When he opened them, the general remained. But the man beneath the armor stood exposed, damp, and aching with the terrible vulnerability of loving someone deeply.

"Shut it off," he called, louder now. Steadier. "Please. Shut it off."

The air changed with the unmistakable shift of a room when a door closes somewhere out of sight. Sound dulled. The clatter of tools softened, as though wrapped in wool. Even the spray of water seemed to lose its violence, breaking into finer mist as it arced through the air.

Mossy felt it before he understood it.

He lowered his arm mid-gesture, fingers still extended in what had been meant as a command, and turned slowly.

At the far edge of the site, just beyond the tent's open seam, two familiar figures had appeared.

Cordelia regarded the scene with her arms crossed, her posture immaculate despite the chaos below. She did not stand *on* the churned earth so much as hover just above it, skirts untouched by mud or water, her presence registering as a sudden tightening in the air rather than a body taking up space. The spray from the ruptured line bent away from her as though unwilling to make contact.

Mossy was the only one who reacted.

Beside Cordelia, Bithia inclined her head, her form less sharply defined, edges soft as candle smoke. Her gaze moved steadily over the damage—the fractured line of concrete, the rising panic among the workers, the way Mossy himself had gone very still, shoulders drawn as if he were bracing against disappointment. She observed without judgment, a quiet anchoring in the midst of noise.

Cordelia drew a sharp breath.

"This," she said, her voice slicing through the moment with unmistakable authority, "is intolerable."

No one else reacted to the words—but the noise faltered all the same.

A contractor froze mid-shout, blinking as though he'd forgotten what he was about to say. Another glanced over his shoulder, frowning, then shook his head as if a sudden chill had passed through him. The water's roar stuttered for half a second before surging on.

Mossy swallowed.

"Cordelia," he said quietly, managing a bow that came from habit more than dignity. "I was just—"

She raised a hand.

"Do not explain," Cordelia snapped. "I can see quite clearly what has occurred."

Her gaze flicked to the ruptured sprinkler line, the water spilling unchecked into the foundation. Then—briefly, unexpectedly—to Mossy's face.

Something shifted.

It was subtle. A loosening at the corners of her mouth. The smallest easing of the line between her brows.

"Well," she said after a moment, with a displeased sigh, "one cannot leave a heart in such a state."

Bithia moved without ceremony.

She crossed the site in a way that suggested distance meant very little to her, her form passing through the cluttered space as if the ground recognized her presence and made room. Her skirts hovered above the splintered planks. Her hem did not stir the dust. She simply *arrived* at the edge of the concrete and lowered herself, the gesture precise.

She did not touch the surface.

Instead, she hovered her hand just above it—close enough that the air between shimmered faintly, as though remembering warmth.

The effect followed at once, though nothing about it was dramatic.

The frantic vibration in the ground eased. The wet churn slowed. The concrete settled, smoothing its own edges as if recalling its purpose. As though reassured that it had not been abandoned mid-creation.

Bithia exhaled—a sound felt rather than heard—and inclined her head.

Hold.

Cordelia stepped forward.

She turned her palm, fingers slightly curved, as though adjusting the position of something delicate.

The air responded.

A focused wind swept across the site. Purposeful. It skimmed the surface of the pooled water, lifting it into a fine, shimmering veil that vanished almost as soon as it rose. Droplets disappeared faster than physics would have allowed, leaving behind darkened earth and cooling stone.

Pixies shrieked with delight as the breeze passed them, caps flying, wings fluttering wildly.

"Formation!" Bumbles shouted.

Mossy blinked, then pushed his glasses up his nose. "Well," he said mildly, "that's handy."

The sprinkler line sputtered once... then fell silent.

Mossy exhaled a breath he hadn't realized he'd been holding.

The heart shape remained.

Not perfect—there would be smoothing, correction, careful tending—but unmistakable. Whole.

He stepped forward slowly, boots squelching slightly, and rested his hand on the stone hippo's broad rump. The statue was cool beneath his palm, solid and absurd and reassuringly present.

"My thanks," Mossy said, the words catching slightly as they left him. "Truly."

Cordelia regarded him with a look that suggested gratitude

was an awkward but tolerable habit. "Thanks are unnecessary," she said. "This ground has been shaped with purpose. One does not abandon a work begun in devotion—particularly not for the lady who holds the key."

Mossy straightened at that, his hand pressing briefly to his chest.

Bithia's expression softened. She turned her gaze toward the house, though she did not look at its walls so much as *through* them. "Nan has given this place an imprint of her own," she said quietly. "In gesture. In care. In welcome. It is fitting that the grounds should answer in kind."

Cordelia nodded once, decisive. "In life, we guarded this house," she said. "In death, we continue. You and Nan now share that charge, whether you recognize it or not."

Mossy swallowed. "I only wished to give her something worthy of her."

Cordelia sniffed. "See that you finish it properly."

Then, as though embarrassed by the sentiment, she turned away.

Mossy nodded, throat tight. He cleared it and straightened, shoulders squaring as though he were addressing a gathered assembly.

"This," he announced solemnly, gesturing toward the heart-shaped foundation, "is sacred ground. It is being shaped not for vanity, nor spectacle, but for devotion. For a woman who has filled a house with warmth, patience, and astonishingly good muffins."

Pixies applauded enthusiastically.

Brash attempted a salute and fell over.

Rufus leaned in. "Breathe," he murmured.

Mossy inhaled. Exhaled.

The noise of the site slowly resumed—measured now and cautious, as though the space had been reminded to behave.

Cordelia cast one last critical look over the area. "See that you finish promptly," she said. "I will not tolerate further disturbances."

And with that she turned away, skirts already fading into the thinning air.

Bithia lingered a moment longer, offering Mossy a small, knowing smile before following.

The tent brightened. Sound returned.

The work continued.

And the heart—steadied and protected—held fast.

Mossy became aware of the phone before he noticed the person holding it.

It hovered at the edge of the tent, angled just so, its lens trained on him like an unblinking eye. He blinked back, momentarily unsure whether exhaustion had finally produced hallucinations.

Then the phone dipped and a voice followed.

"Oh my God!" the voice said, delighted and breathless. "This is *everything*."

Mossy turned.

She stood just beyond the canvas flap, half in sunlight, half in shadow, wrapped in an oversized mustard-yellow sweater that hung off one shoulder as though it had given up on structure altogether. Gold hoop earrings swung as she moved, catching the light with every nod of her head. Her hair—short, blonde, and artfully undone—looked like it had been styled by ocean air.

The phone was already back up.

"Iconic," she murmured, circling slightly to get a better angle. "Raw. Coastal. Authentically unhinged."

Mossy cleared his throat.

"I beg your pardon?"

She lowered the phone at last and smiled—wide, bright, a little frayed at the edges. Up close, he could see it now: the faint shadows beneath her eyes, the way her energy ran just a shade too fast, like someone powering themselves on caffeine alone.

"I'm Jessie," she said, already stepping forward, already talking. "Jessie Dane. I run *Jessie Goes Wandering*. Travel, lifestyle, places with soul. My agent said I need more authenticity and fewer infinity pools, so—" She gestured broadly at the site. "I booked a weekend here."

Mossy glanced down at himself.

Concrete splattered his galoshes. His vest bore a pale handprint. The hard hat had slipped entirely askew, and his hair—usually a thoughtful silver cloud—was plastered in rebellious tufts.

"Well," he said politely, "You are most welcome to our abode, Jessie."

She laughed, quick and genuine. "You're the poet husband, right? That's how social media describes you."

He paused.

"Yes," he said. "Yes, I suppose I am."

Behind him, pixies applauded. One attempted a somersault, misjudged the landing, and vanished into a bucket with a damp *plunk*.

Mossy turned, already shifting out of general and into host. He caught Rufus's eye and inclined his head with exaggerated solemnity.

"Rufus," he said, "I leave the field in your capable hands."

Rufus straightened, adjusted his pilfered hard hat, and gave a crisp nod. "I accept this grave responsibility," he said. Then, after a beat, added, "Bring sandwiches when you return. Lemonade if the sun keeps up. And something with pickles if you're feeling generous."

Pixies erupted at the word *sandwiches*.

"Bread!" shouted Bramble.

"Cold meat!" cried Brash.

"Cucumbers!" Tansy sang, spinning midair.

Mossy smiled despite himself. "Very well," he said. "Try not to conquer anything while I'm gone."

Rufus saluted with two fingers and a pencil. "No promises."

Only then did Mossy step aside and offer Jessie a small, courtly bow; the kind that suggested he'd once taught poetry and never quite stopped performing it. "Allow me to formally welcome you to the Nettles B&B. I'm Mossy. May I carry your bags for you?"

Jessie hesitated. "Honestly?" she said. "That would be amazing."

Mossy gathered the bags—lighter than expected, clearly packed by a woman used to being on the go—and turned toward the house. His boots left pale, imperfect prints behind him, a trail of evidence he made no effort to erase.

Jessie followed, her phone tucked away at last, gaze drifting toward the shaded porch and the open door beyond. Toward quiet, whether she knew it yet or not.

Behind them, the site settled. Pixies resumed their work with renewed purpose. Cordelia watched from the tent's edge, expression unreadable but for a single, approving nod. Bithia's gaze lingered on the departing pair, calm and knowing.

Mossy crossed the threshold of the B&B, still dusted with concrete and battlefield pride, carrying a guest toward rest.

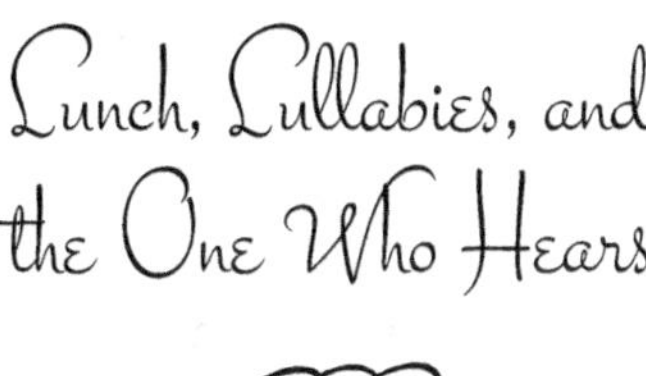

The grandfather clock in the parlor cleared its throat and announced noon with confidence.

Twelve measured chimes rang out, each one rich and steady. Though the count was immediately ruined by pixies swinging gleefully from the pendulum and shouting things that bore no relationship to time at all.

"Seven!" cried Bramble.

"Tuesday!" yelled Brash.

"Twelve and a half!" Tansy added, spinning herself dizzy.

Nan paused in the doorway just long enough to assess the situation, then clapped her hands once.

"Lunch," she said, with the sort of authority that came from years of feeding guests.

Pixies scattered, darting toward the dining room like confetti with wings.

Nan stepped forward, smoothing the edge of the tablecloth as she went. The linen lay crisp beneath her palms—cool and reassuring. She adjusted a fork that had drifted half an inch off alignment—Neat watched approvingly from the centerpiece—and lifted the lid from the soup tureen.

Steam curled upward, rich and fragrant.

"Mushroom and chardonnay," she announced, ladling carefully. "It tastes best if you don't rush it."

Maren clasped her hands. "Oh, Walter, smell that."

Walter leaned in obligingly. "Smells like effort," he said, which Nan took as praise.

She moved down the table, filling bowls, passing flat-breads, sliding glasses of lavender-mint iced tea into waiting hands. Sunlight caught the silver as she went, flashing briefly at her wrist, her rings, the polished curve of the tureen.

Jessie had already positioned her phone.

"Okay, friends," Jessie murmured into it, adjusting the angle. "This is lunch at the Nettles B&B. Everything is house-made, seasonal, and—Nan, where did you get the mushrooms?"

"Two blocks inland," Nan replied without missing a beat. "From a man who insists on cash and tells terrible jokes."

Jessie grinned. "Iconic."

At the far end of the table Maren had leaned close to Walter, whispering something with conspiratorial delight. Walter nodded, unfolded his napkin, refolded it, and placed his newspaper neatly beside his plate, where it would not interfere with soup.

Mossy sat near the window, spoon paused midair. The clatter from outside rose and fell—voices calling out measurements, metal tapping metal.

"All is well," he murmured, more to Nan than anyone else. "Entirely under control."

Nan smiled at him and set the dessert tray just out of reach, where it could be admired without temptation.

Pixies wove happily between chair legs, wings humming like small engines. Bitter darted in, snatched a crumb with a victorious squeak, and vanished beneath the tablecloth. Neat paused to straighten a napkin that had been set a hair off-center, nodding to himself before zipping away. Tansy perched atop the daffodils and sneezed, sending a fine cloud of pollen into the air.

"Bless you," Nan said warmly.

Tansy bowed, one hand pressed to her chest.

Across the table, Maren blinked as the pollen drifted down. "Oh!" she laughed. "I thought I saw a butterfly in there."

Walter nodded agreeably.

Jessie glanced up from her phone, squinting. "Could be lens flare," she said, already scrolling.

Nan took her seat at last, lifting her spoon. Around her, conversation bloomed—about the drive down, the soup, the flowers, and the strange but pleasant feeling of being somewhere new.

For a few heartbeats, the world narrowed to clinking cutlery and murmured approval.

Outside, the work continued.

Inside, the table held.

A knock came softly, as though whoever stood on the other side of the door was prepared to apologize for existing.

Nan got to her feet at once.

"Just a minute!" she called, already moving toward the hallway. Timing, she had learned, was rarely accidental in a house like this.

When she opened the door, the woman on the porch smiled as if she weren't entirely certain she was welcome.

She had auburn curls that had surrendered to the coastal air—springy, unruly—catching light wherever it touched them. A soft cardigan hung open over a faded concert T-shirt. Jeans, sensible brown loafers. Everything about her suggested comfort chosen carefully.

"I'm sorry," the woman said quickly. "I hope I'm not interrupting."

"Not at all," Nan replied. "You're right on time."

The woman blinked at that, then smiled again—this time with relief.

"I'm Deadra. Deadra Price."

Her hands moved as she spoke, shaping small arcs in the air like someone marking time without realizing it.

"Come in," Nan said, stepping aside. "We were just sitting down for lunch."

Mossy appeared at her shoulder, already reaching for Deadra's bag with the instinct of a man who had carried many things for many people and enjoyed the simplicity of the act.

"I'll take that," he said gently. "Your room's just upstairs."

Deadra hesitated, then let go. "Thank you."

She followed Nan into the dining room, pausing just long enough to take in the table, the guests, the flowers. Her gaze moved slowly, as though she were listening with her eyes.

"I'm sorry to be late," she said as she took the offered seat. "The drive was... longer than I expected."

"It always is," Maren said cheerfully. "You think you're nearly there, and then suddenly you're very much not."

Walter nodded in agreement. "Traffic."

Jessie glanced up from her phone. "Are you checking in today?"

Deadra smiled. "I am."

"And what brings you to Daytona?" Maren asked, already leaning forward, interest engaged.

Deadra considered the question for a moment.

"I needed to be near the ocean," she said finally. "And I wanted to be somewhere that I could gather my thoughts. Somewhere I didn't have to explain myself."

Nan felt that land.

"I taught orchestra," Deadra went on, fingers moving again, tracing invisible patterns along the edge of the table.

"Middle school. Twenty years." She smiled faintly. "It's louder than you'd think."

Jessie winced sympathetically.

"There were budget cuts," Deadra said. "And meetings. And forms. And fewer and fewer reasons to remember why I loved it." She shrugged, light and practiced. "I don't teach anymore."

Nan set a bowl of soup in front of her. "You're very welcome here. There's inspiration around every corner."

Deadra looked up at that. "Thank you. I could use some... Inspiration, that is."

Her gaze drifted then past Nan's shoulder, toward the parlor.

Toward the cello.

Nan followed her eyes.

"Oh," Nan said lightly. "That. I found it in the attic this morning."

Deadra's attention stayed fixed on it. "It's beautiful."

"Yes," Nan agreed. "I was just... playing around with it."

Deadra smiled, something old and tender crossing her face. "Do you play?"

"No, not really." Nan hesitated. "But I was drawn to it."

Walter cleared his throat. "You played earlier," he said. "Sounded nice."

Maren clasped her hands. "You must play again!"

Jessie nodded enthusiastically. "Yes, please."

Mossy had returned and settled into his chair, unfolding his newspaper. "Proceed," he said mildly. "What is meant to sound will sound. The rest can wait."

Nan glanced at Deadra.

Deadra nodded once, eyes bright and attentive.

"I'd love to hear," she said.

The room leaned forward.

Nan rose without ceremony and went to the cello. She

simply settled it against her shoulder as naturally as one might gather a shawl. The chair accepted her. The bow followed her hand without argument.

She drew the first note.

It bloomed warm and rounded, fuller than she expected, as though the cello had been waiting patiently for permission to speak. The sound didn't rush outward. It unfurled. A ribbon of tone slipped into the parlor, threading itself between chairs and table legs, brushing against porcelain and linen and skin.

Nan saw it then. Or perhaps *felt* was the better word.

The melody moved like something alive. It drifted, curved, gathered. It settled over shoulders and along spines, coaxing rather than commanding.

Maren was mid-sentence—something about rosemary and childhood holidays—when the sound reached her. Her words loosened and fell away. Her hand found Walter's sleeve and stayed there, fingers curling as though remembering a familiar shape. Walter's posture softened, the careful lines of him easing. His chin dipped, not in sleep yet but in agreement with a thought he no longer needed to finish. The folded newspaper slid from Mossy's fingers and came to rest against his knee.

The music passed over Jessie next. Her camera continued its quiet hum as her eyelids fluttered. She smiled faintly, the practiced brightness easing into something unguarded, and leaned back in her chair, still holding the frame as though the moment might take care of itself.

Nan watched the melody move on.

Teacups tipped just enough to kiss their saucers before growing still. Cutlery settled. Breath slowed. A pixie perched on the dessert tray curled neatly into the curve of a saucer. Another tucked himself into the daffodils, pollen dusting his hair like sleep.

The music gathered them. Wrapped them. Gently laid them down.

Then it reached Deadra.

Nan felt the difference at once.

The melody didn't pass over her. It went *in*.

Deadra's breath deepened. As though her lungs had reached their full capacity. Her shoulders rose slightly, then eased. Her hands, resting in her lap, twitched—just once—as if shaping a chord only she could hear.

The music didn't settle her.

It *woke* something.

Nan's bow slowed. Her heart gave a small, startled beat.

The melody continued to move through the room, but now Nan could see its choice. How it softened and stilled the others, how it lingered with Deadra, threading itself closer, brighter, more intent.

Nan felt her face warm.

Oh.

That was new.

Oh dear.

She kept playing, guiding the melody toward something that felt like an ending. Polite. Brief. A tidy conclusion to an experiment that had clearly proven… effective.

Nan finished the phrase and let the bow rise.

The room held.

Everyone slept, except Deadra.

She looked at Nan with something bright and unguarded in her expression—joy, perhaps. Or contentedness.

"I'm sorry," Nan whispered, mortified. "I seem to have a knack for—well. This. Putting an audience to sleep."

Deadra shook her head gently. "No," she said. "I've been to countless recitals. I know a bored audience when I see one. That's not what's happening here."

Nan glanced around the table. Mossy snored once, softly, then stilled again.

Deadra's hands moved as she spoke, shaping the air as though outlining invisible measures. "How does it feel when you play?" she asked, curiosity pooling in her eyes.

"It feels like the music is already fully in the air all around me and simply needs a vehicle to enter this world."

Deadra considered this.

Nan continued. "I don't know anything about composers," she admitted. "Or technique. I couldn't tell you what key I'm in."

Deadra smiled at that. "I could. I used to." She paused. "I spent years teaching children how to hold their bows. Where to place their fingers. How not to rush the rests." Her voice softened. "Somewhere along the way, I forgot why it mattered."

Nan nodded. "Sometimes a song comes on the radio," she said, "and suddenly I'm twenty-five again. Or standing in my mother's kitchen. Or dancing in a room that no longer exists." She shrugged. "Music has a way of transporting you out of the now and into countless memories."

Deadra's breath caught—as though something had finally reached its mark.

"Yes," she said. "That's it. It takes us out of ourselves."

They sat in the quiet together, surrounded by sleeping guests and the faint scent of tea and flowers. Above them the house seemed to listen, beams and walls attentive in a way Nan had learned to trust.

Deadra's gaze drifted toward the cello.

Nan didn't know why Deadra was different.

But she knew—without doubt—that she was.

Devotion, Disaster, and Drowsiness

By late afternoon, the side garden had entered what Mossy privately classified as *the heroic phase*.

The cement trucks were gone, trundled off like exhausted elephants. And in their place stood the bones of the thing: the heart-shaped foundation, poured and holding, its curves unmistakable even beneath tarps and caution tape. Industrial fans roared at full volume, angled with surgical precision, blasting warm air across the surface in relentless waves.

The tents strained under the pressure. Canvas snapped. Ropes shuddered. Pegs groaned in the earth.

Mossy stood at the center of it all, gripping his clipboard like a battle standard.

"Steady!" he called, raising one arm as though the fans might heed him. "Steady and constant wins the day."

Rufus stood shoulder-to-shoulder with him, hard hat tipped back, knee brace firmly adjusted, eyes narrowed against the wind. He had a pencil behind one ear and squinted toward the curing concrete with the seriousness of a man assessing troop morale.

"Fan three is drifting left," Rufus reported. "That's either a calibration issue or a philosophical disagreement."

Mossy nodded gravely. "Adjust the angle. No existential crises today."

The lawn was covered in cats.

Covered.

They lounged atop overturned buckets and coiled extension cords. They stretched in the sun-warmed dust. They slept in unison, tails flicking occasionally as if responding to some private signal. A ginger sprawled belly-up beside the hydrangeas. A black-and-white pair shared a tarp like old friends.

Mossy waved his clipboard vaguely at them. "I don't understand it," he muttered. "No one sends invitations. They simply... arrive."

"That's Mabel," Rufus said. "She emits a frequency."

Pixies zipped low across the lawn, riding cats like noble steeds. One had fashioned a thimble helmet. Another waved a blade of grass like a banner.

"For valor!" shouted Brash, astride a dignified tabby who blinked slowly and seemed to enjoy the game.

"Sir Whiskerhelm claims this territory," Bitter announced, clutching fur with reverence.

The cats accepted all of it with saintly patience.

Mossy sighed. "At least someone here understands discipline."

Then he looked up.

Nan stood on the front porch.

The white latticework framed her like something out of a fairytale. Sunlight filtered through the cutwork, casting lace-shaped shadows across the boards. She had brought the cello out with care and placed the black lacquer chair just so—angled toward the garden, legs steady, mother-of-pearl inlay catching the light.

Mossy felt the moment land.

She smoothed her skirt. Settled herself. Lifted the bow.

Mabel sat on the white wicker porch swing nearby, gardening apron still tied, hands folded in her lap. She leaned back, listening already, eyes soft, the swing creaking once before growing still.

The fans roared. The tents strained. Dust rose in small spirals.

Nan began to play.

The sound carried, warm and sure—threading through the chaos without effort. It slipped between the fans' thunder and the snapping canvas, moving like a calm hand laid over a fevered brow.

Mossy's chest tightened.

This, he thought, *is why*.

Not the shape of the pool. Not the perfection of the pour. But this moment—her there, music in her hands, his world bending just enough to listen.

He swallowed and squared his shoulders.

"Hold the line," he told Rufus quietly.

Rufus glanced at the porch, then back at the curing heart. "Always," he said.

Behind them, a cat purred. A pixie saluted. And the concrete—blessedly—did exactly what it was meant to do.

Jessie did not so much arrive as *reappear*.

She swept into the side yard through the gap in the tent flaps, phone already in hand, tote slung over one shoulder, gold hoops catching the light as she turned her head. The oversized sweater she wore—soft as a cloud—had one sleeve pushed casually to the elbow, as if she'd dressed for comfort and momentum in equal measure.

She paused just long enough to take it all in.

"Oh," she breathed, and the word carried the pleased

certainty of someone who genuinely enjoyed being surprised. "This is… phenomenal."

Rufus leaned toward Mossy. "That the vlogger you helped in earlier?"

Mossy nodded. "Indeed."

Jessie smiled, and stepped closer—respectful of the work space, eyes bright with curiosity.

"I have to say," she called over the machinery, "your B&B is delightful—but *this*?" She gestured at the tent, the forms, the carefully guarded concrete heart. "This is where the action is."

Mossy wiped his hands on a cloth and smiled. "I'm very glad you're enjoying your stay. Settling in well?"

"Wonderfully," Jessie said. "Though I do seem to have impeccable timing."

She hesitated then—just a beat—and lifted her phone slightly. "Would you mind if I filmed for a moment? An interview, perhaps? Only if it's all right."

Mossy considered this with the gravity of a man weighing both hospitality and destiny.

"Well," he said at last, "I've never been interviewed mid-pour before. But life does seem to reward courage."

Jessie grinned. "I'll take that as a yes."

She angled the phone upward, her voice shifting smoothly into its professional brightness.

"Hi," she said. "Jessie here. And today I've stumbled upon something I can only describe as cozy-core meets… civil engineering."

A pixie riding a cat raised both arms in triumph.

Mossy inclined his head, more windblown than formal. "Welcome," he said. "You've caught us in the act."

Jessie's eyes sparkled. "Okay—first question. Are you always like this?"

Mossy blinked.

"Like... devoted?" he asked.

Rufus snorted.

She gestured toward him with one hand and the entire yard with the other. "Determined. Focused. Slightly heroic. Wearing a fluorescent vest like it's ceremonial."

Mossy glanced down at his vest, which had twisted on his shoulders and was currently flapping in the wind like a pennant. "One does what one must," he said solemnly.

Jessie laughed. It wasn't a mean laugh. It was the laugh of a woman who had stood on enough train platforms, docks, and mountain paths to recognize a moment worth pausing for.

Rufus cleared his throat loudly, as though announcing that the interview had an approved chaperone.

Jessie pivoted toward him immediately. "Oh my gosh. You're the friend. The sidekick."

Rufus's chin lifted. "Second-in-command."

"Respect," Jessie said, nodding like she meant it. Then she turned back to Mossy, phone steady. "Okay—tell me the origin story. How does a poet end up... overseeing a construction site that is overrun with cats?"

"Ah," Mossy said, brightening at the word *poet.*

Jessie's eyebrows rose. "You are a poet. Yes? I read that on the website."

"I am," Mossy confirmed. "Retired professor. Devoted husband. Occasional whisperer of sonnets into the morning air."

She grinned. "That tracks."

Mossy adjusted his glasses, which the wind had tried to relocate to his forehead. "As for this," he said, gesturing toward the tents and the chaos, "this is a grand birthday undertaking."

Jessie's gaze darted to the porch. Nan sat poised in a black lacquer chair, cello tucked close, bow in hand. She looked like a painting someone had commissioned for the sheer joy of beauty.

Jessie lowered her phone an inch. "That's Nan."

Mossy followed her gaze, and something steady and luminous settled behind his ribs.

"That," he said softly, with the reverence of a man naming a constellation, "is my true North."

Jessie glanced at him, surprised into stillness.

"Nanette Nettles," Mossy went on, because once he began he rarely stopped himself. "Dreamer. Baker of impossible breakfasts. Keeper of keys and kindness. She listens to houses the way other people listen to weather. She believes in beauty as a daily practice."

"She is the light by which I have oriented my life," he added gently. "Everything else is just... scenery."

Jessie brought the phone back up. "And you're building her something."

"A gesture," Mossy said. "A love letter in water and stone."

"I see," Jessie breathed, and her tone went reverent as if she were filming a cathedral. "That's... extremely my content."

Rufus muttered, "Content is a strange religion."

Jessie heard him and laughed again, then turned back to Mossy with sudden focus. "Okay. You're a retired professor. You're a poet. Nan plays cello on the porch like she's been doing it forever. Your best friend is wearing a pickleball shirt and a hard hat. Cats have formed an informal party in the grass. And I can't help noticing"—she angled the phone slightly so the heart-shaped foundation filled the bottom of the frame—"that this is a heart."

Mossy lifted his clipboard a little higher. "Yes."

Jessie's voice softened, sharp with curiosity. "Do you always build your love in shapes people can see?"

Mossy stared at her for a moment. Then he smiled.

"You are clever," he said.

Jessie's grin turned quick and pleased. "I travel alone. You either become clever or you become lost."

"Where have you been?" Mossy asked, because it was the sort of question that scratched deeper than the surface.

Jessie's eyes lit. "Okay, highlights." She ticked them off with her free hand, each place spoken like a bead on a string. "Lisbon. Marrakech. Reykjavík. Kyoto. Edinburgh. Mexico City. I did a solo rail trip across Canada once—Vancouver to Toronto—and I cried in a diner in Winnipeg because the waitress called me 'hon' and I hadn't heard anyone say that in weeks."

Mossy's face softened. "A diner blessing," he murmured.

Jessie laughed. "Exactly."

"And in Lisbon," Mossy said, warmed by the list, "Pessoa would have approved of your solitude."

Jessie blinked. "Fernando Pessoa?"

Rufus's head snapped toward Mossy. "Oh no."

Mossy continued calmly, as though quoting European modernists at a construction site was perfectly ordinary. "He wrote of being many people at once. A traveler becomes many selves. The self on the airplane is not the self on the cobblestones."

Jessie's eyes widened, delighted. "Okay," she said, voice bright. "You're not just poetic. You're a walking library."

Mossy inclined his head. "I do my best."

Jessie turned slightly, phone still up. "In Marrakech I thought of Rumi, obviously. Reykjavik—Halldór Laxness, though I'm still working through him. Kyoto made me quiet. Like... haiku quiet."

Mossy's mouth curved. "Bashō would approve."

Jessie snapped her fingers. "Bashō." She pointed at him like he'd just won a round. "Yes. *That* energy."

Rufus leaned into Mossy, stage-whispering, "I do not know what is happening, but I feel outmatched."

"Edinburgh," Jessie continued, warming to the exchange, "was all fog and poetry and old stone. I sat on Calton Hill at dawn and tried to pretend I was in a Brontë novel. Which is impossible, obviously, because I had a granola bar and a phone charger."

Mossy laughed. "The modern heroine."

Jessie nodded gravely. "Exactly."

Mossy tilted his head, curiosity brightening his expression. "Tell me—why the Brontës? Edinburgh is a bit far from the moors."

Jessie smiled, pleased by the question. "I know," she said quickly. "They belong to Yorkshire. Wind and heather and all that." She gestured vaguely, as if summoning a landscape. "But Calton Hill at that hour—before the city really wakes—had that same feeling. Like the world was holding its breath. Like if you stood still long enough, the wind would whisper a story of long ago into your ear."

Mossy's smile softened. "Ah," he said. "The atmosphere of longing. The terrain of interior weather."

"Yes!" Jessie said, pointing at him. "That. Exactly that."

Rufus, who had been listening with great seriousness, nodded once. "You've both described pickleball mornings perfectly."

They looked at him.

Rufus shrugged. "Foggy. Quiet. Full of hope and bad dinks."

"And yet," Mossy said, catching her tone and returning it with gentle precision, "the yearning remains the same."

Jessie paused, phone still, eyes on his. "That's... true."

The wind tugged at the tent wall hard enough to make the ropes twang. A contractor shouted something about measurements. A cat yawned with theatrical boredom. Pixies scampered along a plank, giggling, one of them attempting to place a tiny leaf on Jessie's shoulder like a medal.

Jessie didn't flinch. She simply kept looking at Mossy, thoughtful now, the humor still there but quieter.

Mossy's hands tightened on his clipboard. For a moment he was aware of the fans, the concrete, the heart shape under tarps, the schedule slipping like sand. He was aware of the way he'd woken with joy and then spent hours wrestling logistics.

Then he heard Nan's cello.

The notes drifted across the yard, threading between the machines and the voices, slipping into spaces where the wind couldn't tear them apart. The sound carried warmth. A steadiness that resonated deeply.

Mossy's shoulders eased.

Nan's bow hand moved with calm assurance. Her posture looked effortless, as if the cello had always belonged to her. Mabel sat on the porch swing, head tipped slightly, listening with a softness that made her look younger.

A moment later, Mabel's eyelids lowered.

Her head drifted toward her shoulder.

The porch swing creaked once... twice... and stilled.

Mossy's smile faltered.

Jessie's voice softened, the question returning as if she hadn't finished it. "So, Mossy... what happens when you finally reveal the surprise?"

Mossy turned back to her to answer—

—and saw her blink slowly, like someone waking from a dream in reverse.

Her eyes fluttered once. Twice.

She swayed slightly, phone still held upright with stubborn professionalism.

Jessie's mouth opened, but the sentence wandered off before it reached daylight.

Then she leaned—gently, almost gracefully—straight into the hydrangea bush beside her, as if the blossoms had called her by name.

Her phone kept recording.

A pixie gasped in awe.

Another whispered, "Art."

Mossy stared, mortified, then hurried forward. "Miss Dane? Jessie?" He crouched beside the hydrangeas. "Are you unwell?"

Jessie exhaled a small sound of contentment and smiled faintly into the leaves.

Rufus stepped closer, peering down. "She's asleep."

Mossy's cheeks warmed. "I bored her."

Rufus looked at him as if Mossy had suggested the ocean was dry. "You quoted Pessoa in a wind tunnel beside a heart-shaped pool foundation. That woman asked you about beauty and exhaustion. You did not bore her."

Mossy blinked, still staring at Jessie's peaceful face framed by hydrangea petals.

Rufus nodded toward the porch. "Also," he added, lowering his voice, "your wife is playing the cello again."

Mossy turned his head.

Nan's music drifted through the air, soft as a hand at the back of a neck.

Mossy swallowed.

"Oh," he murmured.

A cat rolled onto its side and fell asleep mid-stretch.

A pixie riding that cat toppled gently into the grass and immediately began snoring.

Mossy stared at the yard full of sleeping creatures and one perfectly unconscious travel writer, and the truth hovered close enough to touch.

He simply hadn't taken hold of it yet.

Not with the fans roaring.

Not with the heart curing.

Not with the day pressing forward like a marching drum.

He rose, brushing dust from his vest with distracted care. "Rufus," he said softly, "would you... keep an eye on her?"

Rufus nodded. "I'll guard the hydrangea. With honor."

Mossy tried to gather his composure, his gaze drifting back to the porch where Nan played.

Mabel slept on the swing with a faint smile.

The notes carried on.

And Mossy, standing in the wind with devotion in his chest and chaos at his feet, felt his eyelids grow heavier than they had any right to be.

He blinked.

Once.

Twice.

The world felt... softer. As though someone had turned the volume down.

Jessie slept in the hydrangeas, phone still clutched in her hand, her expression peaceful in a way no influencer ever looked while awake. Rufus stood nearby with his arms crossed, watchful as a sentry, though even he swayed faintly on his feet.

Across the lawn, cats lay everywhere—on stones, on garden edging, on one another. Pixies curled among them like ornaments fallen from a parade float. One pixie used a cat's tail as a blanket. The cat purred louder.

Beyond them, the construction crew had succumbed as well.

One worker slumped upright in a folding chair, hard hat tipped forward over his eyes, arms crossed like a man determined to nap responsibly. Another laid stretched along a stack of lumber, vest glowing fluorescent against the wood, one boot dangling off the edge as though he'd simply paused mid-thought. A third had folded himself improbably into the cab of the work truck, chin resting on the steering wheel, mouth open in peaceful surrender.

Even the foreman—clipboard still clutched in hand—leaned against a tent pole, snoring softly, his pen marking slow, drifting arcs down the page.

Safety vests rose and fell in gentle unison.

The entire battlefield had gone blissfully, inexplicably still.

Mossy frowned. This felt... excessive.

He shifted his weight, leaned a shoulder against the tent pole, and told himself very firmly that he was not tired.

That was when the air changed.

Quieter—like a held breath.

Bithia hovered just beyond the reach of the fans, her form catching the light without interrupting it. Cordelia appeared beside her, hands folded, posture precise even in half-transparency.

"Mossy," Cordelia said crisply, "you are witnessing a pattern."

Mossy squinted at her. "Mm. Patterns. Yes. Roman roads were marvels of—"

"This is not about roads," Cordelia snapped.

Bithia gestured with one gentle hand. "The cello," she said. "It carries a rest enchantment. A remembering spell. It eases bodies into stillness."

"Sleep," Cordelia added. "Uninvited. Indiscriminate."

Mossy nodded solemnly, eyelids lowering. "That explains Rufus's lemonade tasting like chamomile."

"It must be broken," Cordelia continued. "Or guided. Left unchecked, it will blanket the house."

Bithia leaned closer, urgency soft but unmistakable. "Someone hears it differently. Someone stays awake. You must watch for that."

"Yes," Mossy murmured. "Watchful. Vigilant. Like a centurion." His head tipped back against the canvas.

Cordelia's mouth tightened. "He's drifting."

"I am not," Mossy said, eyes fully closed. "I am merely... resting my thoughts."

"You are snoring," Cordelia said.

Mossy adjusted his stance, one hand sliding to his chest.

"Nan deserves fountains," he mumbled. "And swans. Two. No —three. The third is symbolic."

Rufus sighed from somewhere far away.

Bithia watched Mossy with fond resignation. "He loves her very much."

"That," Cordelia conceded, "is his most redeeming quality."

Mossy smiled faintly in his sleep. "Veni… vidi… nap-vi."

The music drifted on from the porch—steady and warm. Unhurried.

The house listened.

And the warning, spoken clearly and kindly, settled gently into the afternoon—

unheeded, for now.

The House That Would Not Wake

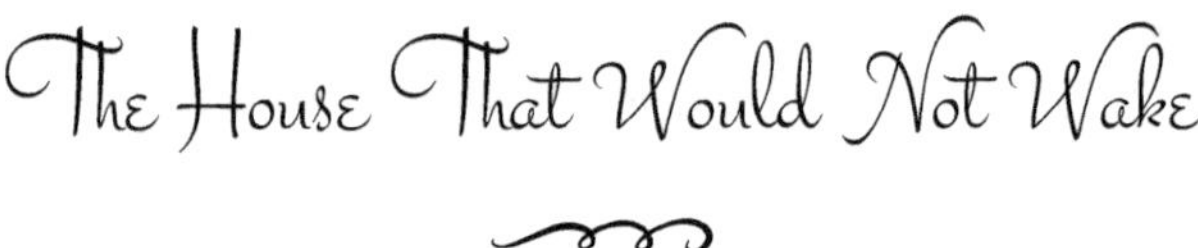

Nan lowered the bow.

The final note didn't vanish so much as *settle*, like a held breath finally released. It lingered in the air a moment longer than sound ought to, then folded itself neatly into the afternoon.

The porch went quiet.

Quiet in a way that felt... deliberate.

Nan rested the cello against her knee and looked up.

Mabel slept on the porch swing, her knitting abandoned mid-row. One needle had slipped free and dangled from the yarn like a thought she'd meant to finish later. Her chin tipped toward her chest, mouth slightly open, curls stirring in the breeze. The swing creaked once then stilled, as though it had decided not to interrupt.

Beyond the porch rail, the side yard was scattered with cats.

Not gathered sensibly, the way cats sometimes did. These were arranged with a peculiar creativity—one draped over a flat stone like melted butter; another sprawled belly-up in the mulch, paws in the air as if surprised by sleep. Two laid nose-to-nose beneath the hydrangea, tails touching. A calico had chosen the very center of the stepping path and appeared unwilling to negotiate passage.

Nan frowned mildly.

"Well," she said to no one in particular, "this is quite something."

She listened.

No rumble of machinery.

No shouted measurements.

No metallic clatter or thud.

The construction sounds were *gone*. As if someone had reached out and turned the volume knob all the way down.

Nan shifted the cello, careful of its weight. The bow rested loosely in her right hand.

It shivered.

Just once—a small, unmistakable vibration, like a cat purring at a distance you could feel more than hear.

Nan stilled.

She waited for the feeling to pass. It did not.

Curious now rather than concerned, she lifted the bow again and drew it lightly across the strings.

The sound came easily. Warm, rounded. It opened the air instead of pressing against it, moving outward like light through clean glass. Nan felt it move through her chest and shoulders, down her arms, settling somewhere just behind her eyes.

She felt awake.

Not sharp-awake, the kind that came with lists and timers and responsibilities, but a gentler alertness. As though she were standing inside a dream that had decided to let her keep her awareness.

She glanced at Mabel.

Nothing.

Mabel slept on, untroubled by music, magic, or curiosity.

Nan played another phrase. The sensation deepened—pleasant, steady, anchoring—but nothing changed beyond her.

The cats didn't stir.

The porch didn't sigh.

The swing didn't creak.

Nan lowered the bow again.

"Oh," she said softly.

The word wasn't alarmed. It wasn't even surprised. It was the sound she made when she noticed a recipe had behaved differently than expected, or when bread rose a little higher than usual.

She stood, lifting the cello with care. The instrument felt warm against her side, as though it had been soaking in the sun. The bow hummed faintly in her grip. Attentive.

Inside, the house greeted her with silence that had weight to it.

Nan paused just past the threshold.

The parlor was full of people unmistakably asleep.

Walter sat in his chair with his glasses still perched on his nose, hands folded over his stomach. Maren leaned sideways against the table, cheek resting on her knuckles, smile caught halfway through enthusiasm.

None of them looked unwell.

They looked... *finished*.

Nan stepped carefully between chairs. The floorboards didn't creak. Even the house seemed to be minding its manners.

In the corner a throw blanket had slid halfway to the floor, frozen mid-fall. A teacup sat abandoned with a ring of steam still clinging faintly to its rim. Someone—she suspected Mossy—had left a page half-turned in the newspaper, the crease hovering undecided.

Nan moved through the room slowly, the cello tucked close.

She felt the same alert warmth she had on the porch. It didn't fade indoors. If anything it sharpened, her senses tuning themselves to the space around her. The house didn't feel empty of sound so much as *full of listening*.

She stopped near the base of the stairs.

Everyone was asleep.

Everyone except her.

Nan looked down at the cello.

The varnished surface caught the light differently now, as though the room had adjusted itself around the instrument. The bow's faint vibration had stilled but the sense of readiness remained, a quiet expectancy humming just beneath the surface.

"Well," she said softly, more to the house than the instrument, "you're up to something."

She didn't name it. Didn't reach for conclusions. Nan had learned long ago that some things preferred to introduce themselves in their own time. She trusted that Anton and the cello were doing something needed. Something magical.

She rested the cello carefully against the wall and stood still in the parlor, listening.

Footsteps touched the stairs, measured, as though whoever descended already understood the tone of the house and intended to match it.

Deadra appeared at the turn of the banister.

She looked rested—not freshly awakened but *returned*. Her auburn curls had settled into themselves, softened by sleep and humidity into a shape that felt honest rather than arranged. She wore jeans and a loose cardigan over a faded concert tee, the kind that had been washed thin with time. Her shoulders were relaxed. Her eyes were clear.

They went straight to the cello.

Her hands rose without her noticing—fingers curving slightly, shaping air as though an invisible bow waited there. Her breath slowed, then matched something Nan could not hear.

Deadra stopped at the foot of the stairs, taking it in.

"You played again," she said quietly.

Nan nodded.

Deadra smiled. Something inside her eased, like a door left ajar at last. "I could tell," she said. "The house sounds... muffled."

"Tea?" Nan asked, keeping her voice low.

"That would be lovely," Deadra said, and followed her into the kitchen with careful steps, as though she were being invited into the inner sanctum.

The Nettles kitchen glowed with late-afternoon light. Wide windows let the sun spill across butcher-block counters worn silky from decades of use. Copper pans hung along one wall, catching soft reflections. Jars of flour and sugar lined the shelves beside neatly stacked mixing bowls, their rims nicked and familiar. A faint sweetness lingered in the air—vanilla, citrus peel—the memory of something baked not long ago.

Nan moved with quiet assurance. She filled the kettle and set it on the stove, its lid settling into place with gentle certainty. When the water warmed she poured slowly, steady hands guiding the stream into waiting cups. Steam rose in delicate curls, carrying the clean scent of tea leaves and warmth.

Deadra leaned against the counter, watching. Her shoulders eased further with each small sound—the ceramic cup set down, the spoon resting against the saucer, the soft breath Nan released.

Nan slid a mug toward her. "Careful. It's hot."

Deadra wrapped her hands around it, closed her eyes, and smiled.

Deadra moved toward the cello, not touching it. Her eyes

traced the curve of its body, the way the light caught along the varnish.

"It's older," she observed. "Antique-old. Lived-in old. You can tell by the wear along the ribs. That doesn't come from storage."

"I found it in the attic this morning."

Deadra glanced at her, surprised. "This morning?"

"Yes."

Deadra crouched slightly—not touching, just looking closer. "The varnish has been reworked at least once. Carefully. Someone loved this instrument enough to keep it breathing." Her gaze shifted to the bow resting nearby. "And that thumb cushion—see? That's not factory. That's someone noticing pain and deciding to do something about it."

Nan watched her, struck by the gentleness of her attention.

"You know a lot," Nan said.

Deadra shook her head. "Not really. Just observant."

She straightened, wrapped both hands around her teacup, and leaned against the back of a chair. Her voice stayed low.

"I taught orchestra," she said. "Middle school. Twenty years." She smiled faintly. "I was very good at it. Organized. Patient. I could tune a room full of sixth graders in under two minutes."

Nan smiled back.

"But somewhere along the way," Deadra continued, "music stopped being the inspiration and became just a method. Schedules. Fundraisers. Budget meetings. Parents asking why their child wasn't first chair." She took a sip of tea. "I stopped playing. Told myself it was temporary."

Nan didn't interrupt.

"Temporary stretched," Deadra said. "Then my marriage ended. Quietly. No explosions. Just... drift." She glanced around the room. "I came here because I needed quiet. I needed a place where nothing was asking anything of me."

Her gaze returned to the cello.

"I wasn't looking for music," she said. "But it seems everywhere I look, there it is."

Nan felt it then—the distinction she'd been circling.

Deadra met the sound with wakefulness.

The music gathered her inward instead of carrying her away. Presence settled into her, gentle and sure.

Nan watched the way Deadra's shoulders rose and fell with her breath, how her fingers gave a small, unconscious flutter, as though remembering their work. The spell—if that was what it was—curved around her, attentive rather than possessive. Leaving her anchored fully in herself.

"You don't seem sleepy," Nan said gently.

Deadra smiled. "I feel... rested. As if something I've been holding very tightly decided to set itself down."

Nan nodded. She understood that kind of relief.

They sat together in the quiet, two women holding teacups, surrounded by sleeping guests and a listening house.

Nan looked once more at the cello.

Then at Deadra.

She said nothing. Some things were better carried forward than spoken aloud.

The feeling stayed with her.

Nan drew the chair into place and settled the cello between her knees, the familiar weight fitting her perfectly. She adjusted the angle and let her breathing find its rhythm.

She moved the bow across the strings and let the sound come, gentle and curious.

The first note slipped free, low and careful, like a question asked without expectation. The sound moved through the house immediately—settling deeper into the rooms where sleep had already claimed its territory. Somewhere down the hall, a chair creaked as a body shifted further into rest. The hush thickened, gentle and complete.

Nan kept her movements small. Respectful.

The music behaved as it had before—curling, soothing, drawing the edges of the house inward. It passed through walls and doorways with practiced ease, threading itself into the beams and banisters like breath into lungs.

And yet—

Deadra remained.

She sat at the kitchen table, eyes open, expression softened but alert. The sound didn't fold her inward. It didn't cradle her toward sleep. Instead, it seemed to pause when it reached her—hovering and attentive, as though waiting to be answered.

Nan felt it then. Clear as heat against skin.

The music was speaking.

Deadra's breath slowed with focus. Her hands rose slightly, palms angled, fingers curving in shapes learned long ago. When she spoke, it was in a whisper.

"It's an old instrument," she said. "You can hear it in the way the sound blooms instead of pushing. That kind of resonance comes from years of being played by someone who listened as much as they performed."

Nan lowered the bow, letting the final note settle where it wished. "I don't know its history," she admitted. "I don't know composers or techniques. I just know..." She searched for the words then smiled softly. "I know how it makes me feel. Like a song on the radio that pulls you straight back into another life. Another kitchen. Another version of yourself."

Deadra nodded slowly. "That's the part we forget," she said. "When music becomes schedules and lesson plans and budgets. When you're correcting posture more than feeling sound." Her voice stayed steady, but something in her eyes shimmered. "I used to tell my students music was a language. But I stopped speaking it myself."

Silence gathered between them.

Deadra took a step closer. Then another.

Her hand hovered just short of the cello's curved shoulder. She didn't touch it. Just looked.

"I didn't come here looking for this," she said quietly. "I came to rest."

"Sometimes," Nan said just as softly, "rest comes from remembering what we loved before we were tired."

Deadra's fingers brushed the wood.

The contact was brief. Solemn.

Her breath caught with surprise and tears followed without warning. She pressed her lips together then shook her head once, as if startled by herself.

"I'm sorry," she said, already stepping back. "I just—"

"There's nothing to apologize for," Nan replied.

Deadra nodded, wiped her cheeks with the heel of her hand, and managed a small, grateful smile. "I think I need a moment," she said. "If that's all right."

"Of course."

Deadra slipped away toward the stairs, her steps light and cautious.

Nan remained in the kitchen, the cello warm against her side.

She ran her thumb along the bow's grip, feeling the faint hum still waiting there.

"Well," she murmured to the quiet house, to the listening walls, to the instrument that had chosen its response carefully, "we'll sort this out together."

Wrong Put Right

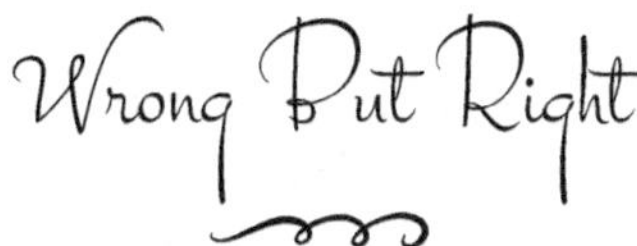

The pool was almost full.

That was the first thing Mossy noticed—the waterline inching upward, glistening against the pale tile like a clock that had decided to measure time in inches instead of minutes. The fire hose roared as if offended by the task it had been given, its thick black body bucking slightly where it disappeared over the edge of the pool, water blasting in with unapologetic force.

Firefighters were everywhere. Boots soaked. Sleeves rolled. Helmets abandoned in a cluster near the hedge like shed exoskeletons. Someone had propped a ladder against the tent pole and was leaning on it with the loose-limbed posture of a man who had done his part and was now enjoying the spectacle.

"I still say this doesn't count as an emergency!" one of them shouted over the rush of water, shielding his face as a gust of mist caught him full in the chest.

Another laughed. "Tell that to the guy whose wife is turning seventy today."

Mossy flinched and checked his watch.

Too late.

Not *past* late. Worse. *Almost* late.

Which was the most treacherous time of all.

He tilted his head back and squinted at the sky. The sun hovered above the tree line, smug and orange, as if it had all the time in the world.

"It's setting," Mossy announced to no one in particular.

A firefighter glanced up. "It is not."

"It's absolutely setting," Mossy insisted, tapping his watch as though it might corroborate him. "I can feel it in my bones."

"That's humidity," Rufus said cheerfully, appearing at his elbow with a grin that suggested he was enjoying himself far too much. "Sun's got at least an hour."

"An hour?" Mossy repeated faintly. "That's barely a thought."

Behind them a pixie shrieked with delight as she mounted the fire hose mid-surge, wings flaring as she clung to the rubber and let herself be dragged along in a wild arc of spray.

"Do not—" Mossy began.

Too late.

She whooped and slid, hair plastered to her face, landing in a wet heap near the edge of the pool. Two more pixies followed immediately, one standing upright like a rodeo rider, the other hanging upside down and waving enthusiastically at a group of firefighters who didn't seem to notice.

"Is this," one of them asked slowly, "normal?"

Another shrugged. "I think it's a fundraiser?"

"We don't fill pools," a third muttered, hands on hips. "We fight fires."

"Yes," Rufus said pleasantly, "but you *lost* at pickleball."

A groan rippled through the group.

"That was one game," someone protested.

"That was *three* games," Rufus corrected. "And the Chief said—and I quote—'Winner gets a favor'."

Mossy closed his eyes briefly and pressed two fingers to the bridge of his nose.

Of course.

"History will not remember the pickleball match," he reflected, watching the fire hose thunder into the pool. "But it may yet remember Rufus, who spent his one favor not on glory—but on Nan."

A pixie saluted a firefighter from atop a cat who had wandered into the chaos and immediately decided to lie down in the damp grass.

"Hold the line!" Mossy heard himself say, though he wasn't entirely sure which line he meant.

Rufus clapped him on the shoulder. "You're doing great."

"I am not," Mossy replied. "I'm conducting an orchestra composed entirely of improvisation."

Rufus considered this, watching a firefighter sidestep a ladder while a pixie zipped past on the hose. "I think they call that jazz."

Mossy froze.

Jazz.

"Yes," he said slowly, the word settling into him. "Of course. Jazz. No score. Just timing and trust. One man keeps the beat, another wanders, a third pretends he knows where he's going and somehow... it works."

He swept a hand toward the scene—the water rushing, the shouted instructions, the laughter, the overlapping motion. "That hose is percussion. The shouting is brass. Everyone listening for the moment they're needed."

Rufus nodded, pleased. "I like jazz."

Mossy smiled despite himself, something easing in his chest. He checked his watch again.

Still almost late.

The smile vanished.

"Which means," he said, straightening, "we are entering the dangerous part of the song."

To his left the white party tent billowed softly, its fabric catching the breeze like a sail that had already committed to the journey. Mossy didn't remember exactly when it had gone up—only that at some point it had existed, pristine and luminous, as if conjured by will alone.

He stared at it.

Beautiful.

Terrifying.

"Nobody let Nan see," Mossy murmured.

"She won't," Mabel said calmly, appearing at his side without warning.

She carried a spool of ribbon tucked under one arm, and the serene authority of someone who had already decided this would work.

She turned her head and addressed a pair of staff members struggling with a ladder.

"Lanterns higher—no, higher than that," she called. She tilted her head, considering the line of lights against the sky. "Yes. Like they're about to take flight."

The ladder shifted. The lanterns were lifted. The yard seemed to exhale and rearrange itself around her certainty.

"See?" she said to Mossy. "She won't peek. She never does when she's meant to be surprised."

"How do you know?" Mossy asked.

Mabel didn't look at him. "Because today she wants to be surprised."

Mossy swallowed.

People moved around them in every direction. Staff carrying trays. Firefighters stepping aside to avoid cats. Pixies weaving through legs like glittering hazards. Someone bumped into someone else, apologized profusely, then bumped into another person immediately.

Mossy felt his pulse in his ears.

He loved this woman. He loved her so fiercely it made him foolish. He had planned poetry and water and beauty and intention. And now here he was, ankle-deep in chaos, watching firefighters argue with one another about hose etiquette while the hose itself bucked and veered as if possessed.

A pixie slid past on a sheet of spray, whooping.

One of the firefighters frowned at the nozzle. "I swear this thing just pulled."

"Hydraulics," another said doubtfully.

Mossy closed his eyes for half a second and chose not to correct them.

He checked the sky.

"It's setting," he said weakly.

"It is not," five voices replied at once.

The waterline kissed the tile edge.

The fire hose roared on.

And Mossy, overwhelmed and wide-eyed, saw the truck before he saw the problem.

It idled across the street with patient menace. The side panel read:

Swamp to Shore Exotic Birds & Events

The lettering had once been cheerful. Now it was sun-faded and flaking at the edges, portions peeling as though the truck had grown tired of pretending it offered balloons and chair covers.

A man leaned against the driver's door, with a faded blue ball cap clutched in one hand. He was mid-argument on his phone, voice sharp over the roar of the fire hose.

"Darla, I'm telling you, I didn't *promise* 'two swans and a vibe'. I promised two swans and—" He glanced at the Nettles property, where the side yard had become a choreography of urgency. "—whatever this is."

Mossy's stomach tightened with the particular dread that came from recognizing a sentence in progress and knowing it would not end in your favor.

Rufus appeared at his side as if summoned by that exact frequency of trouble. His hardhat sat at a jaunty angle; his vest had acquired a constellation of damp spots. His face wore the calm of a man who had accepted that today's reality was mostly improv.

"Is that... ours?" Rufus asked.

"It is," Mossy said softly, as though speaking too loudly might make it real. He checked his watch, because watching time pass felt marginally more productive than watching the universe conspire. "And it is late."

"Maybe it's early," Rufus offered.

"It is not early," Mossy replied. "Nothing in my life has ever been early."

The fire hose continued to thunder water into the pool, which was almost full. Firefighters stood around it now with the relaxed air of men who had accomplished something they weren't supposed to be doing and were already drafting the story they'd tell later.

Mossy turned his gaze back to the bird truck.

The day required swans. The day demanded swans. The day, he suspected, had been built in part on the symbolic dignity of two white birds gliding across a heart-shaped pool like a dream.

He exhaled slowly and looked at Rufus.

"Rufus," he said, voice low with the solemnity of a man issuing battlefield orders, "I require you to go across the street and retrieve two swans."

Rufus nodded once, like a knight receiving his quest.

"Two," Mossy emphasized. "Swans. White. Elegant. Aristocratic."

"Got it," Rufus said, already stepping away.

Mossy grabbed his sleeve.

"And Rufus," he added, narrowing his eyes as if trying to press the instructions directly into his skull, "only the purest of white. No black swans for this day."

Rufus looked offended on principle. "Mossy," he said, "I know what a swan looks like."

Mossy held his gaze for a moment.

"Excellent," Mossy said politely. "Good man,"

Rufus strode toward the *Swamp to Shore* van with the confidence of a man who had never been humbled by a bird.

Mossy watched him go and felt, briefly, the warmth of something like gratitude. Rufus could have used his one favor with the fire chief on anything—car trouble, a fallen tree, a mysterious smell in the garage that should not be investigated without professionals.

And he had chosen this.

He had chosen Nan's birthday.

"Gallant," Mossy murmured, and tipped his chin as if Rufus could hear the benediction from thirty yards away.

A hand touched his elbow—human, warm, and firmly practical.

Mabel appeared beside him. "You're making that face again," she said.

"My face is doing what it must," Mossy replied. "It is the face of a man who has planned a perfect evening and is now watching the day behave like a feral kitten."

Before Mabel could respond a van turned into the drive with a confidence that suggested it had never once worried about space, timing, or the sanity of its surroundings.

It bore the logo of a catering company—gold script, elegant and self-assured.

The van rolled past a coil of hose, past a ladder, past a firefighter who raised a brow at it as though the universe had just delivered the next act of a play he'd been forced to attend.

The van stopped.

The driver's door opened.

And out stepped a chef in a crisp jacket, smiling like this was all exactly as planned.

"Bonjour!" the chef called, which felt like an unnecessary flourish in Florida, but Mossy respected commitment.

Behind him, two more men emerged and opened the back doors of the van.

Mossy braced himself.

They began to slide out something enormous.

Not a tray. Not a cart.

A pan.

A pan so large it could have hosted a small baptism.

Four men appeared—no one knew from where, only that the universe provides when it wishes to witness spectacle. And together they wrestled the thing onto a rolling stand with the reverence of a ceremonial object.

The pan wobbled once.

A firefighter winced, hands moving instinctively as if he might need to catch it.

Mossy's heart performed an abrupt leap.

The pan was steadied.

The chef beamed.

"This," he announced, gesturing as if unveiling a masterpiece, "is paella for your party. Feeds one hundred and fifty people."

Mossy stared at it.

His brain attempted to find language, failed, and attempted again.

"That," he managed, "appears to be... for the entire county."

The chef laughed, delighted. "Ah! You are generous host, yes?"

Mossy nodded slowly.

His mind reframed in self-defense.

This was not dinner. This was opulence.

He could already picture Nan's face when she saw it. The way her eyes would widen, then soften. Then she'd laugh, because she would find beauty even in absurdity.

Mossy opened his mouth to ask practical questions like *Where will we put it?* and *Is it supposed to steam like that?* and *Why does it smell like the ocean married paprika?*

But a shimmer of motion at the edge of the pan caught his attention.

Pixies.

They'd gathered at the rim like curious children at a fountain, their tiny bodies glowing in the humid air, attention fixed on the rice with gluttonous hunger.

One pixie—Bramble, naturally—darted forward and plunged both hands toward the paella.

Another froze mid-hover, eyes wide, voice hushed with awe.

"We have fallen into shadow."

Before Mossy could intervene—or philosophize about the metaphor—Mabel swept in.

"Absolutely not," she said briskly, appearing between pan and pixie with her yard stick raised like a shield. "This is *dinner*, not a rite."

She flicked a look at the chef. "Serving table goes *there*—yes, along the hedge, thank you. You'll have room to breathe, and the guests won't wander."

The chef nodded at once, relieved to be handed certainty, and began redirecting his team.

Mabel leaned closer to Mossy, her voice dropping just enough to be kind.

"I've got it, darlin'."

Mossy exhaled. Fully. Completely.

Behind him, a low sound of alarm surfaced.

Rufus had returned from the bird truck—empty-handed for the moment—and stopped short at the sight of pixies, paella, and Mabel in full command.

"Oh," he said thoughtfully. "Good. I missed something."

A firefighter watching the chef's team set up the pan leaned toward his buddy and murmured, "Is that... seafood?"

His buddy squinted. "I think it's art."

Mossy swallowed a laugh.

He had no time for art. He had time only for whatever came next.

Which was, unfortunately, the next thing.

A second vehicle pulled in—a smaller van this time, white with pink lettering. It stopped too close to the hose.

Mossy's eyes narrowed.

The back doors opened.

And out came the baker carrying a cake box that looked like it might contain a small building.

The baker was sweating, face flushed with the effort of moving something heavy and sacred through chaos. He nearly tripped over a coil of fire hose, corrected himself with an athletic hop, and beamed as though this was an everyday obstacle in his profession.

"Cake delivery!" he announced.

Mossy felt a wash of relief.

Yes, he thought. *The crowning jewel.*

Then the baker set the cake down on the nearest table and opened the box.

Mossy leaned forward.

Time slowed.

The cake emerged with ceremony.

It was tall—impressively so—its tiers stacked high and iced in thick, glossy swirls that caught the afternoon light like lacquered porcelain. The color palette announced itself immediately: riotous bands of purple, green, and gold spiraled around the cake in unapologetic celebration, threaded with draped strings of edible beads cascading down the sides like they'd been flung there mid-parade.

Mossy blinked.

"This," the baker announced proudly, bracing the stand as if it might attempt escape, "is a King Cake."

The chef paused mid-step. A firefighter stopped chewing. Even the air seemed to lean in.

"And," the baker continued, lifting one sugar-dusted finger with ceremonial gravity, "there is one alligator baked inside."

Mossy opened his mouth. Closed it again.

On the very top of the cake stood the *second* alligator.

He was upright. Regal. Entirely unapologetic.

The figurine wore a tiny black top hat tipped at a rakish angle and held a slender gold cane mid-swing, one foot kicked forward as if caught forever in the act of dancing. His tail curled with flair. His grin suggested jazz. Possibly rebellion.

Beads looped around his neck and spilled down the tiers in festive excess. Sugar glitter caught in the folds of the icing. The cake announced celebration.

The baker beamed. "Whoever gets the gator inside wins."

"Wins *what*," Mossy asked faintly.

The baker considered. "Glory," he decided. "Bragging rights. The prize itself."

Mossy stared at the cake.

Rejected it.

Reconsidered.

Then something warm and unmistakable settled in his chest—the quiet click of recognition.

"King Cake?" he said slowly, shaking his head with a smile that spread all the way to his eyes. "No. This is a *Queen Cake*."

The baker paused. "Is it?"

"Oh, absolutely," Mossy said, straightening as if the matter were now settled law. "It's her birthday."

Somewhere near the table, unseen but unmistakably present, pixies erupted into delighted chaos.

"LONG LIVE THE QUEEN," they chanted, tiny voices rising in triumph.

Mossy looked once more at the dancing alligator, the beads, the color, the audacity of it all—and felt his worry loosen its grip.

He pictured Nan, seventy years old today, laughing in the parlor. He pictured her delight in the ridiculous. He pictured the way she adored anything that felt like Florida giving her a wink.

And he pictured Rufus, somewhere out there, earnest and well-meaning, doing his best to retrieve aristocratic birds from a truck whose logo was long past its prime.

Mossy exhaled.

Then, with the solemnity of a man accepting destiny, he nodded.

"Yes," he said. "That is... perfect."

The baker's face brightened. "It is?"

"It is," Mossy affirmed. "It is... profoundly correct."

Mabel appeared, took one look at the alligator topper, and made a noise that sounded suspiciously like joy.

"Oh, Nan is going to love that!" Mabel exclaimed, already stepping in beside the baker.

"That goes right here, darlin'," she said, steering the baker toward the long cake table beside the multi-tiered punch fountain. "Careful now—yes, right there. Plenty of room to admire."

The punch fountain burbled softly, liquid amethyst cascading from tier to tier.

Mabel paused, head tilting. "Oh, look at that," she added pleasantly. "The purple punch will match fantastically."

Mossy raised a finger, suddenly earnest. "We are not saying the phrase *'Nan is going to'* in my presence right now. I cannot handle future tense."

Mabel patted his arm without looking at him. "Then breathe in present tense."

She breathed in deeply and exhaled slowly.

"I've got this, darlin'."

And somehow—miraculously—Mossy believed her.

Then.

Rufus returned, walking toward them carrying two large cardboard pet carriers with air holes punched in the sides.

Mossy's brows rose.

"Ah," Mossy said, forcing calm. "Excellent. Swans."

Rufus smiled proudly. "Swans," he confirmed.

Mossy stepped forward and opened the first carrier.

A duck stared back at him.

Mossy blinked.

He opened the second carrier.

Another duck stared back.

This one tilted its head as if evaluating Mossy's leadership qualities.

Mossy closed both carriers slowly.

He looked at Rufus.

Rufus looked back.

A long moment passed in which Mossy's soul attempted to leave his body and was called back by duty.

"Rufus," Mossy said very softly, "these are ducks."

Rufus's smile faltered only slightly. "They're... fancy ducks."

Mossy inhaled.

He prepared a lecture.

He knew he was preparing a lecture.

He could not stop himself.

"Ducks," he began, lifting one finger, "are members of the

Anatidae family. They are practical birds. Adaptable. Resourceful. Unlike swans—which are, arguably, symbols of devotion and grace and—"

He paused and glanced toward the pool. Imagined two swans floating like a dream.

Then he looked back at the carrier.

The duck stared at him with unwavering confidence.

Mossy's finger dropped.

His shoulders softened.

Perhaps, he realized, the trick was not controlling the day but loving it when it refused to behave.

"Fine," he said, and the word held surrender and affection both. "We shall have ducks."

Rufus brightened instantly. "I knew you'd come around."

Mossy shot him a look. "Do not interpret this as encouragement."

Rufus already was.

Mossy waved a hand. "Release them. Carefully. With dignity."

Rufus popped the latches.

The ducks waddled out like they owned the side yard, took one look at the nearly full pool, and headed toward it without hesitation.

Mossy watched them go with the numb awe of a man who had stopped questioning the universe.

The pixies, of course, reacted immediately.

They swarmed toward the ducks like a parade.

One pixie produced a tiny crown made of woven grass and placed it proudly atop the larger duck's head.

Another pixie climbed onto the duck's back and raised an arm as if steering a grand vessel.

The duck accepted this leadership without question.

It stepped into the pool water with imperial calm.

The second duck followed, a pixie clinging to its feathers like a knight mounting a horse.

Mossy watched the regatta begin—pixies giggling, ducks gliding, water shimmering—and felt the first true laugh of the afternoon break loose in his chest.

Mabel leaned in close, eyes bright. “You see?” she murmured. “You’ve got this darlin’.”

Mossy looked at the pool—nearly full, nearly finished, nearly ready.

He looked at the paella pan gleaming like a feast for royalty.

He looked at the alligator Queen Cake waiting proudly for its moment.

He looked at the ducks accepting pixies.

And somewhere beneath the chaos he felt it: a thread of beauty tightening into place.

“Hold the line,” he murmured again, but this time he knew which line he meant.

The sun was still in the sky.

The pool was filled.

The day was disobedient.

And Mossy was bending to it.

“Alright,” he said to himself, to the house, to the whole unruly orchestra of preparations.

“Let’s make it sing.”

The Room Before

The upstairs dressing room had been built for a woman of a different era.

For trunks with brass corners and travel stickers from cities where people wore gloves to breakfast. For hatboxes. For velvet wraps that smelled faintly of lavender sachets and steamship air. For the kind of life that required a room devoted entirely to mirrors and the careful choosing of who you intended to be when you stepped back out into the world.

Nan paused in the doorway and imagined it as it once had been—Bithia and Cordelia here together, corsets loosened, hairpins scattered across the vanity, silk gloves laid out in pairs. A last sip of tea before the opera. A shared glance before the carriage ride. The quiet, conspiratorial pause that always came before a woman became visible again.

Some rituals, she realized, did not belong to any single century.

They lived when women gathered like this—behind the scenes, shoes kicked off, shoulders bare, laughter softening the air. Preparing not just to be seen but to step into the world together.

Light poured in through tall windows dressed in pale, sweeping drapery—soft blue and silvery gray, gathered and pinned like a ballroom gown caught mid-twirl. The sea sat beyond the glass, steady and shining, as if it had been invited to illuminate the moment.

A chandelier hung overhead in a riot of crystal, dripping brilliance onto everything below. Two long vanities faced one another beneath arched mirrors, their gilt frames catching the sun and tossing it back in warm, flattering flashes. The walls were painted a dignified, dreamy blue with gold detailing at the edges. As though the room had once belonged to a minor European countess who loved lipstick and loved herself even more.

Now the room belonged to women who loved tea, and laughter, and the relief of taking their shoes off.

A tufted ottoman sat in the center like a polite little stage. A chaise curved beneath the windows, upholstered in blush velvet and piled with pillows that looked as if they'd never heard a harsh word in their lives. A soft rug anchored the room, pale and ornate, and it muffled footsteps until every movement became a secret shared between friends.

Champagne waited in two silver buckets, the bottles sweating like they'd run upstairs in a hurry to make it in time. Flutes gathered in small, cheerful clusters among makeup brushes, perfume bottles, stray earrings, and silk wraps. A ribbon spool sat near a compact mirror, a hairpin glinting near the edge of a jewelry tray like a tiny fallen sword.

Nan stepped inside and felt—at once—how the room held her.

Not like a hostess.

Like a woman.

Jessie sat at the far vanity with her phone propped against a perfume bottle as if it belonged there. She wore a blush-pink sequin dress that caught the light in quick, playful sparks whenever she shifted her weight. The dress made her look like she'd been poured into celebration—soft pink shimmer, delicate straps, the kind of fabric that moved like a sigh.

But Jessie's voice—usually bright and fast and determined to capture everything—moved differently today.

She spoke into the lens in a hush, like she was talking in a library.

"I can't believe I landed here this weekend," she murmured, turning the camera slightly so the chandelier drifted into frame. "This is... a literal dressing room fantasy. And we are getting ready for the proprietress's seventieth birthday." She breathed out a small laugh. "Seventieth."

Nan noticed the way Jessie filmed now—less frantic, more deliberate. As though she had decided this moment was worth keeping exactly as it was, without commentary or rush.

Nan felt a small, familiar fondness. She had once been that young woman, collecting moments like proof that life was happening.

Only the tools had changed.

Her own early years lived first in photographs taken by others—film developed slowly, moments returned weeks later. But *her* memories, the ones she claimed as her own, lived in square Polaroids, colors softened by time. Birthday cakes tilted toward the lens, friends caught mid-laugh, Mossy perpetually half out of frame because he was always the one taking the picture and never thought to step in front of it. Those photographs lived now in thick albums, the kind with peeling black pages and careful white corners, her handwriting looping beneath each image: *summer, first apartment, don't forget this.*

Later came rolls of film dropped at pharmacies, envelopes of glossy prints she sorted at the kitchen table while dinner cooled. Later still, digital cameras—Mossy obsessive as ever, uploading, labeling, saving everything twice "just in case". He had digitized her life, scanning decades into neat folders without ever throwing the originals away. *You never know what you'll want to hold,* he'd said.

And now here was Jessie, gathering the present with a phone small enough to slip into a pocket. Yet still pausing long enough to feel the weight of what she was capturing.

Nan liked that. The pause. The choice.

Somewhere along the way, she had learned that memory wasn't about how fast you collected it but about whether you stayed long enough for it to settle. Whether you let the moment mark you, instead of the other way around.

She hoped—without quite knowing why—that Jessie would remember this one not just as footage but as feeling.

Nan had spent a lifetime scanning rooms for needs. Now, with nothing required of her, her gaze simply followed warmth where it gathered.

Maren lounged across the chaise with her heels kicked off, one foot tucked under her knee, the other dangling and swinging lazily like a girl on a porch swing. She wore a navy dress—structured and elegant, the kind of silhouette that made a woman's posture improve without being asked. A slim sash at her waist cinched it into place in a rich burgundy. Her pearls nestled at her throat in layered strands—classic, composed, very *Maren*.

And yet... Nan noticed she looked unhurried.

For the first time since Maren had arrived, she did not look as though she were running late for a life she loved too much to miss. There was no invisible list ticking behind her eyes. No urgency humming beneath her smile. Just presence—settled, and surprisingly sweet.

"Oh good," Maren said, her voice light with genuine relief. "There you are. We were starting to worry we'd dressed up too early."

Nan laughed, the sound rising easily. “I think we are right on time,” she said.

Maren grinned and leaned forward conspiratorially. “I’ll confess—while we were waiting for you we may have snooped a bit. Just a little. One of the trunks yielded something rather lovely, and we thought...” She gestured vaguely toward the room, the Champagne, the women. “Well. We think it’s perfect for this day.”

“I don’t mind at all,” Nan said gently. “I’m still discovering secrets in this house myself. That’s half the joy of it, I think—the finding. The sense that something has been waiting patiently for the right moment to be noticed.”

Maren studied her then, a little quieter. “That’s a very comforting way to live,” she said.

Nan smiled. “I’ve found it’s the only way this house will cooperate,” she admitted.

Deadra turned slightly from the window and the light caught the copper in her curls.

She wore black—one shoulder bare, the fabric draping across her collarbone with quiet grace. The line of the dress fell long and clean, elegant without trying too hard, as if she’d chosen simplicity because she didn’t need to prove anything. A silver bracelet gleamed at her wrist. Her hands kept moving in small, instinctive ways—fingers shaping air, wrists turning gently as though she could feel music even when the room was silent.

She crossed the room before Nan could say another word, her expression bright with the kind of contained excitement that refused to be polite.

“Okay—wait,” Deadra said, already reaching into the curve of her arm. “We really did find something extraordinary.”

She produced a small, oval case wrapped in time-softened leather the color of old cherries. The hinges gleamed faintly.

The lid bore no name—just a discreet embossing, elegant and certain of itself. The sort of thing that had once traveled the world tucked into velvet-lined trunks.

Nan stopped short.

"Well," she said, breath catching with laughter and something like awe, "that looks serious."

Jessie was already moving, phone lifted, eyes wide.

"Okay—no—hold on—this is an *unboxing moment*," she whispered, circling them like a documentarian afraid to miss history. "I love women. I love this house. I love *whatever is about to happen*."

Deadra opened the case.

Inside, nestled against dark silk, lay a tiara—delicate but assured. Pale green stones shaped like leaves arched upward in a soft crown, their color echoing spring just before it turns. Silverwork threaded between them like veins, precise and fluid, the craftsmanship unmistakable.

From the chandelier above Nan felt the familiar flutter—quick, delighted. Pixies spilled from the crystals like sparks shaken loose, wings catching the light as they looped and dove, hands clapped to mouths in delight.

"Ohhh," breathed Tansy, hovering near Nan's shoulder.

"A crown," murmured Bramble, solemn as a courtier.

"For *our* queen," Bitter added, nodding gravely.

Nan blinked, eyes shining.

Deadra lifted the tiara with both hands. "We thought—" she began, then stopped, laughing softly. "Well. We didn't think too hard. It just... felt like you needed it today."

She stepped closer. "May I?" she asked.

Nan nodded, unable to speak just yet.

The tiara settled onto her head as if it had always known where to rest. Cool at first, then warming. Aligning. Just right.

Jessie's voice wobbled behind the camera. "I am *losing my*

mind," she whispered. "This is the most elegant thing I've ever seen that didn't involve a red carpet."

Pixies drifted lower, inspecting, approving. One adjusted an imaginary angle. Another sighed dramatically and pretended to faint midair.

Nan laughed then—soft and delighted, a sound that filled the room. She lifted a hand to the crown, fingertips brushing the stones.

Maren was already on her feet. "Turn," she said, all business now. "Let's see the whole picture."

Nan wore a gown that seemed to have been waiting for this very moment—silk the color of dusk, neither blue nor violet but something in between, skimming her frame with ease. A soft drape at the shoulder revealed her pearls, luminous against her skin, their familiar weight grounding her. Beneath them, a long silver chain traced a quiet line down her bodice, the small key resting warm against her heart. Unassuming, steadfast, and entirely hers.

Mabel emerged from behind the vanity mirror, towel gone, hair now a loose, glossy wave. She took one look and pressed a hand to her chest.

"Oh," she said. "Yes. That's settled, then."

"Well," Nan said at last, voice warm with wonder, "I appear to have been promoted."

Deadra's eyes shone. "Happy birthday," she said simply.

Nan met her gaze, something deep and grateful passing between them.

Above them, the chandelier chimed faintly as the pixies returned to their perches, already telling the story among themselves.

Cordelia and Bithia emerged the way thoughts do when you're very still—already present before you notice them.

The air near the vanity gathered itself. Light bent, then softened. Cordelia resolved first, her form translucent but precise, every line of her posture intact even without weight. She drifted forward, skirts gliding a fraction above the rug, eyes already trained on Nan.

And then—she saw the tiara.

Cordelia's expression changed at once—illuminated. Her chin rose a notch, her shoulders straightened, and something like pride moved through her, quick and unmistakable.

"Well," she said, the word landing with quiet satisfaction.

Bithia appeared beside her, gentler, her presence felt more than seen at first—a warmth at Nan's shoulder, a steadiness in the room. She followed Cordelia's gaze and smiled.

"That was Lady Astor's," Bithia murmured, her voice meant only for Nan. "She gave it to Cordelia after a sitting.

Cordelia sniffed, though the sound held no disapproval. "Nancy Astor was formidable," she said. "Sharp. Observant. Never mistaken about worth." Her gaze remained on Nan. "She would have admired you."

Nan's breath caught but she did not speak.

Instead she lifted her chin slightly, just enough to acknowledge the compliment, and let her hand rest at her waist as if steadying herself. To anyone watching, it would have looked like a woman settling into her jewelry. Only Cordelia saw the flicker of gratitude pass through her eyes.

Bithia's expression softened further. "Jewels," she said quietly, "are meant to be worn. Not forgotten in velvet boxes, waiting for permission." Her gaze lingered on the tiara, pleased. "It's good to see it in the light again."

Nan inclined her head—small, precise.

A thank-you shaped in posture alone.

Cordelia gave a short, decisive nod. "An excellent choice," she said. "For an excellent woman."

Across the room, laughter rose. Champagne flutes clinked. Jessie adjusted her camera angle, entirely unaware that history had just leaned in close.

Nan turned back toward the living, her smile already in place.

Behind her the spirits drifted apart again, their approval lingering like perfume in the air. Present, but known only to her.

Mabel's voice carried from the far side of the room, dry and composed. "Before anyone asks—I am saying nothing."

Every head turned.

Jessie's phone swung toward her instantly. "So that's a yes on surprises," Jessie whispered to the camera.

Maren raised her brows, amused. "We're not asking for spoilers," she said lightly. "Just... general expectations."

Mabel took her Champagne flute—already poured, because Nan knew her so well—and held it aloft like a conductor pausing an orchestra.

"All I will say," she announced, "is that you may wish to thank your past selves for choosing forgiving waistlines."

Deadra laughed outright. "That kind of party."

Mabel nodded. "There will be food. There will be abundance. There may be seconds that pretend to be firsts."

Nan caught the glint in her eye. "Mabel."

Mabel smiled sweetly at her. "Birthday rules," she said. "You are required to have more than one piece of cake."

She took a sip, then added breezily, "And wearing comfortable shoes is never a mistake."

Maren leaned back against the chaise, delighted. "Noted."

Jessie lowered the phone just long enough to grin. "I respect that—but I'm a So Kate girl through and through. One hundred millimeters or bust."

A ripple of amusement moved through the room.

"Oh, I remember that phase," Maren said thoughtfully. "When you believed pain was just part of the silhouette."

Jessie laughed. "It *is* part of the silhouette."

Deadra smiled from where she stood by the window. "It's

amazing what we're willing to endure when we think confidence lives a few inches off the ground."

Mabel laughed then—a rich, unapologetic sound. "Oh, sweetheart. My stiletto days are long over." She lifted one foot just enough to make her point. "This girl is all in on Mary Janes."

Nan grinned. "You did your time," she said gently.

"And enjoyed every minute of it," Mabel added. "I strutted. I teetered. I blistered." She wagged a finger at Jessie, fond rather than admonishing. "Strut it while you've got it, girl. No shame in the shine."

Jessie raised her glass. "To strutting."

"To knowing when to sit," Maren added.

"And to choosing what makes you feel like yourself," Deadra said quietly.

The room burst into laughter—warm, knowing, and generous.

Mabel took a sip, sighed, and then looked directly at Nan with a wicked little smile.

"Mossy is beside himself," she announced. "Absolutely undone. He's convinced you'll peek and ruin the surprise."

Nan's face warmed. "I would never."

Mabel arched an eyebrow. "You would consider it."

Nan opened her mouth, then laughed quietly. "I would consider it with restraint."

Jessie leaned closer to her phone. "The restraint is the brand."

Maren raised her flute. "To restraint," she toasted, and there was a gentle irony in it that made Nan laugh again.

Nan looked around the room, taking in each woman as if she could preserve the moment by seeing it hard enough.

Maren's navy elegance and pearls, softened by ease.

Jessie's blush sparkle, her voice hushed, her eyes brighter

than they'd been earlier—like the day had rinsed the franticness off her.

Deadra's black drape, the steady presence in her posture, her hands remembering music even while she stood still.

Mabel—a force of nature—already preparing to enjoy the evening.

Jessie's voice softened further as she spoke into the camera again. "This is the part of travel that never makes the highlight reel," she said. "The *before*."

Maren's gaze settled on Nan. "Walter went outside," she said casually, fastening her earring at last. "He said Mossy looked like a man trying to juggle time. So he went to see if he could carry something. Or stand in front of something. Or offer moral support by existing."

Nan's chest warmed at that.

Deadra's laugh was soft but genuine. "I heard the cello earlier," she said, voice low as if honoring the hush the house seemed to like these days. Her eyes flicked to Nan. "It did something to me."

Nan's fingers tightened around her flute.

Bithia's gaze drifted toward Deadra. Cordelia's attention sharpened, a needle finding thread.

Nan chose her words carefully, the way she chose dishes for her table—intentionally, not by rote habit.

"The house has been... restful," she said.

Mabel made a pleased sound. "Restful," she repeated, approving. "Yes. That's the word. The whole place feels like a quilt someone pulled up to your chin."

Maren stared at her own reflection for a moment as if she hardly recognized the woman looking back. Then she adjusted her earring and said, quietly, "My mind has stopped sprinting ahead of me."

Jessie's smile faltered into something tender. She took a sip from her glass, eyes shining. "I woke up earlier," she said, and her voice caught on the truth. "And I didn't reach for my phone first."

Nan blinked.

Jessie's mouth tilted with self-mockery. "I know. Please applaud my growth."

Maren leaned forward and clinked her glass gently against Jessie's. "Brava."

Deadra raised her flute, too, and her smile held gratitude that didn't require explanation.

Nan stood among them—among sequins and pearls, among Champagne and mirrors and the hush that had gathered itself in the corners of the house—and felt something inside her settle.

Downstairs, a distant roar rose—water and voices, the sound of Mossy's world in motion.

Up here the women adjusted earrings, smoothed skirts, dabbed perfume at wrists.

Nan took a slow sip of Champagne and let the room hold her.

Cordelia drifted past her shoulder, sniffed approvingly at the scent of perfume, and murmured, as if to herself, "Appropriate."

Bithia's voice followed, soft as a blessing. "Beautiful."

Nan didn't answer either of them aloud.

She simply smiled and winked.

The room began to change its mind about stillness.

Flutes were refilled, then set aside. Earrings were fastened with careful fingers, clasps checked and rechecked by friends who leaned close. Lipstick was blotted away with the pad of a fingertip. Shoes—chosen, debated, laughed over—were finally slipped on.

Someone smoothed Nan's shoulder. Someone else tucked a loose curl back into place.

The door opened.

Warm air rushed up the staircase, carrying laughter and the low hum of voices gathering outside. Somewhere beyond the windows, music drifted—indistinct, festive, already alive. Lantern light flickered against the walls as the women began to move as one, a gentle procession shaped by familiarity rather than plan.

They went ahead of her, one by one.

Jessie last, filming. Maren with glass in hand. Deadra pausing just long enough to meet Nan's eyes, something unspoken passing between them. Mabel sweeping out with a promise of cake and fun.

Nan lingered.

She rested her hand on the banister, fingers curled around the worn wood, and let the house hold her for one last breath. Seventy years pressed softly at her back. A life fully lived. A moment fully arrived.

Then she turned.

The cello waited where she had left it, quiet and expectant.

Nan smiled.

"Well," she stated softly, reaching for it, "you might as well come, too."

She gathered it into her arms and followed the sound of her people down the stairs, carrying the promise of music with her into the light.

Nan did not mind the blindfold.

That in itself nearly undid him.

She stood beside him in the side yard, her arm looped through his, her posture relaxed, chin tipped slightly as though listening to the evening rather than waiting for it. The blindfold—soft silk tied carefully at the back of her head—covered her eyes but not her smile.

"Are you sure you're ready?" Mossy asked for the fourth time.

"Yes," Nan said calmly. "I've been ready since you tied the knot. I'm just curious how long you intend to narrate my birthday like a radio program."

Mossy cleared his throat. He was aware—painfully so—that he had been talking for some time.

"I only mean," he continued, undeterred, "that certain things deserve proper introduction. Context. A sense of... of lineage."

Nan's fingers tightened briefly where they rested over his wrist.

"Mossy."

"Yes, darling?"

"Can I take it off now?"

"Not yet."

She laughed softly, the sound a familiar balm. Somewhere nearby a chair scraped. Cutlery chimed. Laughter drifted, low and contented. Mossy felt the evening holding itself still around them, like a breath drawn and not yet released.

Deadra's presence brushed close—he didn't look, but he felt her. A gentle hand reached in, careful and reverent, easing the cello from Nan's grasp.

Nan's hands lingered in the air a moment longer, fingers curved as if remembering the instrument's shape.

"It's gone," she observed mildly.

"Only for a moment," Mossy said quickly. "Everything is accounted for."

He shifted his stance, squared his shoulders. This mattered. All of it mattered.

"You see," he began, "there are different kinds of love. There is the love that arrives early and stays loud. There is the love that waits. And then there is the love that hardens—not in a brittle way but like cement. A love that sets."

Nan hummed. "Cement."

"Yes," Mossy said, encouraged. "And fowl."

She turned her head slightly toward him. "Fowl."

"Yes," he repeated, more firmly now. "One might say this evening is a love shown in cement and fowl."

Nan laughed, the sound full-bodied and delighted. "I'm going to need that embroidered."

"Now, don't interrupt," he said, fond but resolute. "This metaphor has legs."

"Dearest," she warned, amusement laced with threat, "I am going to peek."

He tightened his grip on her hand. "Please don't."

She didn't but her fingers curled into his; grounding,

anchoring. Mossy felt the shift in her body immediately. He always did. The subtle stillness when something touched her deeply. The way her breathing changed when emotion gathered unannounced.

He needed her to see it all at once.

He needed the moment to land fully formed.

Because Mossy believed fiercely that if love was done properly, it could be seen.

He believed that devotion left evidence.

He believed that effort mattered—not as spectacle but as offering.

"Mossy."

"Yes, my love?"

"You're vibrating."

"I am under control."

Nan's smile widened.

Behind them, someone cleared their throat.

"Mossy," Mabel said, calm as a church bell. "Let her take the blindfold off."

He froze.

He looked at Nan—though she could not see him—and in her covered gaze he found trust. Complete and unguarded.

"All right," he said quietly. "All right."

He reached behind her head and loosened the knot, careful not to disturb her tiara.

The blindfold slipped free.

Nan blinked once.

Then again.

Mossy watched her see.

Firefighters sat at round tables dressed in white linen, sleeves rolled, boots damp, laughter easy now that their work was done. They leaned back in their chairs like men invited not just to a party but to rest. Some held plates already, others glasses raised mid-story.

B&B guests glowed in the lantern light, faces open, bodies settled, conversation flowing without urgency. No one looked at a watch. No one hovered at the edge of leaving.

Lanterns drifted overhead, strung in generous arcs, swaying slightly with the breeze.

Food stretched across long tables in abundance. Steam rose gently. Color, scent, warmth. Enough for everyone and then some.

Nan's breath caught fully.

"Oh," she gasped.

Mossy felt it then—the hum. A rightness.

Her gaze moved.

The pool.

Heart-shaped, as planned. Water dark and luminous, catching reflections of light and flame. Ducks glided across its surface in calm procession, utterly at ease with their role in the evening. Mossy caught glimpses of the pixies darting between them, their tiny hands skimming water, delightful spirals of motion. He felt joy ripple outward.

"And the pool," she continued, wonder threading her words. "It's a heart."

"Yes," Mossy said. And then, because he was incapable of stopping himself now, "well—yes, but also—do you remember the Poconos?"

Nan's head tilted slightly toward him, a smile already forming. "The tub," she said. "The absurdly small heart-shaped tub."

"Precisely," Mossy said, delighted. "Too small for two people, technically. Yet we persisted."

"We overflowed," Nan recalled fondly.

"We did," he agreed. "And we laughed. And you said—very sternly, I might add—that if something was shaped like a heart, it ought to be generous about it."

She laughed softly. "I did say that."

"So," Mossy continued, warming to his theme, "I thought —what if the heart were large enough this time? Not for soaking, but for holding. For floating. For letting things drift." He gestured vaguely toward the water. "A heart that doesn't rush you."

Nan's breath slowed. He felt it beside him, the subtle shift he had learned to recognize over decades.

"And hearts," Mossy went on, because now he truly could not stop, "have always meant more than romance to you. You once told me that a heart wasn't about passion so much as endurance."

Nan squeezed his hand.

"I did say that," she murmured. "You remembered? That was ages ago."

"I remember everything you say when you're holding a glass of wine," he replied solemnly. "It's when the truth sneaks out."

Her laugh brushed against him like silk.

She looked up again, taking in the light overhead. "And the lanterns?"

Mossy followed her gaze. "Ah," he said. "Those."

He shifted closer, lowering his voice as though confiding a secret.

"Do you remember that summer in Provence?" he asked. "The one where the electricity kept failing and the innkeeper insisted it was 'romantic' rather than 'inconvenient'?"

Nan smiled fully now. "You read poetry by candlelight and nearly set the tablecloth on fire."

"Only once," Mossy said. "And you saved it. But what I remember is how the light made everything softer. As though the world was willing to meet us halfway."

The lanterns swayed gently above them, catching gold and amber and pale white.

"And the ducks?" Nan asked, turning back to him with amused affection.

Mossy winced, then rallied. "Yes. The ducks." He cleared his throat. "There were supposed to be swans."

"I see."

"They symbolize devotion," he said earnestly. "Lifelong pairing. Mutual regard. An elegance that borders on the theatrical."

"And ducks?" Nan prompted gently.

"They symbolize adaptability," Mossy said after a beat. "And community. And doing one's best with what is available."

Nan laughed again, and this time it caught—warm, rich, and unmistakably moved.

She turned slowly, taking it all in again: the tables, the people, the light, the water, the improbable beauty of effort layered upon love.

Mossy watched her shoulders lower. Watched the last trace of overwhelm soften into something like peace.

She squeezed his hand once more.

"Mossy," she said quietly, "this is beautiful."

Something in his chest loosened—unwound, really, as though a long-held breath had finally been released.

He stepped closer, guiding her gently forward.

"Come," he said, voice thick now but steady. "There's more. And I want to show it to you properly."

He took her hand and led her—his queen—to the edge of the heart-shaped pool. Where light shimmered, water waited, and the evening stood ready to receive her, carrying with it every memory he had gathered, every story he had shaped, and every quiet truth he had cherished.

She squeezed his hand.

"Mossy," Deadra said gently.

He turned, still half-dazed from the sight of Nan taking in

the pool, the lights, the ducks—still riding the swell of relief that she had loved it. Truly loved it. Her hand remained warm in his, her thumb tracing slow, absent circles against his knuckles.

"Yes?" he asked.

"I heard you tell Nan you'd meant to have swans."

Mossy winced. "Yes. Well. Plans were made. Adjustments occurred."

Deadra smiled in understanding. She glanced toward the pool, where the ducks glided with serene indifference, utterly unbothered by their role as substitutes.

"I can't produce a swan," she said.

Her gaze shifted to the side, to where the cello rested in its stand, polished wood catching lanternlight, quiet as a held breath.

"But," she continued, voice steady now, "I can play *The Swan.*"

No one rushed her. No one clapped. No one filled the space with encouragement or commentary. Sound itself seemed to step back—cutlery was lowered, laughter softened, conversations thinned and drifted away like mist.

Mossy felt it before he understood it.

A tightening in the air. Alignment. The same sensation he'd felt earlier, watching Nan take in the reveal. A rightness settling into place.

Deadra moved toward the cello.

And then—

Mossy saw him.

At first, he thought it was a trick of light. Lanterns swayed, reflections danced across water and glass and polished surfaces. But this was different. This was *presence.*

A man hovered beside Deadra, just half a step back.

He did not cast a shadow, exactly, but the space around him seemed to hold more intention. He was dressed impeccably, though Mossy could not have said in what era. His posture carried the ease of someone long accustomed to listening.

Mossy's breath caught.

Nan felt it instantly.

She tightened her fingers around his hand and leaned closer, her voice barely more than a thought.

"Yes," she murmured. "I see him, too."

Relief washed through Mossy so quickly it left him dizzy.

"All right," he whispered back, blinking. "Because—just for the record—we already have two ghosts in this house, a fluctuating number of pixies, and now apparently an apparition of a cellist."

He swallowed, eyes flicking briefly back to the figure at Deadra's side. "There *is* a limit, Nan. I don't know what it is, but I feel it's important to acknowledge one exists."

Nan's shoulder shook with silent laughter.

"When will it end?" he went on, unable to stop himself. "Am I meant to be keeping a ledger? Do they check in? Is there a sign-up sheet?"

She turned her face toward him, calm as ever, eyes warm.

"Oh, darling Mossy," she murmured. "This one won't stay."

He frowned. "You're sure?"

"Yes," she said softly, certainty threaded through the word. "Some spirits come to linger. Some come to meddle." Her gaze drifted back to the cello, to the man who hovered there with quiet devotion. "And some come only to remind another soul of the art they never truly lost."

"Well," he said faintly, squeezing her hand, "that's a relief."

Nan smiled and rested her head against his shoulder. And Mossy—at last—let go of the need to understand.

Deadra lifted the cello with reverence, as if she were greeting an old friend rather than handling something fragile.

Her hands found their places without searching. The instrument settled against her shoulder, the curve of it fitting her body as though it had been waiting for *her*.

Mossy felt the change before the bow ever touched the string.

Deadra drew it across with calm assurance, no testing note, no clearing of the throat. The sound rose immediately—full, luminous, tender. It unfurled into the night like silk released from a hand.

The music skimmed the surface of the pool, smooth as breath over water, then sank gently into it, sending ripples outward. Lanternlight trembled. The ducks stilled, drifting as if the sound itself were carrying them. Conversation softened—loosened, as though everyone had collectively been lulled to listen.

Nan turned, eyes wide with wonder, and scanned the tables, the guests, the firefighters leaning back in their chairs, the staff mid-step.

"No one's falling asleep," she said, delighted.

Mossy let out a startled laugh. "I should *hope* not," he replied. "It's a party."

But Nan wasn't really listening anymore.

She was watching Deadra.

"Look at her," Nan murmured, awe threading her voice. "How natural she is. Like she never stopped playing."

Mossy followed her gaze. Deadra's face had gone utterly still. Open. Tears slid down her cheeks without disrupting her bowing, without breaking the line of sound. The cello sang.

And there—just there—hovered the apparition that Mossy had decided not to acknowledge.

His expression one of quiet, unmistakable approval.

Mossy felt Nan's fingers tighten in his hand.

"He's smiling," she whispered.

"Well," Mossy muttered under his breath, "I suppose that's a good sign."

Nan shot him a look, fond and steady.

Mossy watched the guests again—and felt it then, unmistakably.

Breaths deepened. Shoulders dropped. Laughter, when it came, sounded richer. People leaned closer to one another without urgency, without the exhaustion that had clung to them earlier like damp wool.

The cello was no longer demanding rest.

It was offering joy, in this quiet music.

Mossy thought of all the lectures he had given over the years, all the poems he had quoted about music's power to soothe, to heal, to order the soul. Plato, Bach, Yeats. *Music as the shorthand of emotion*, he'd once said to a room full of undergraduates who had nodded politely and gone on to forget it.

But this was different.

This was not the easing of weariness; it was the return of motion.

Deadra's bow dipped, danced. The melody rose and fell like breath taken freely after a long confinement. Mossy felt it move through him—not loosening him into sleep but into presence.

He squeezed Nan's hand.

The cello sang on—no longer burdened, no longer asking.

Complete and alive.

Jessie's phone was raised.

"This—" she began softly, then stopped.

She tried again. "You're hearing—"

Her voice trailed off.

The camera lowered.

She stood very still.

Mossy turned to Nan without thinking and extended his hand.

"May I?" he asked.

She smiled the kind of smile that held history in it, and rose.

They stepped onto the small wooden dance floor Mossy had insisted upon, even when everyone told him it was unnecessary. He was suddenly grateful beyond words that he had not listened.

His tux felt different than it had earlier—less like a costume, more like a second skin. The fabric moved easily with him now, no longer stiff with ceremony, as though it had finally understood its purpose. He guided Nan into his arms and she came without hesitation, fitting there as she always had.

They didn't count steps, they simply moved.

Slowly. Together.

Nan rested her head against his shoulder, the familiar weight of her settling into him as natural as breath. Her hand curved at his back, fingers warm through the layers of fabric, and Mossy felt something inside himself ease open. A holding he hadn't known he'd been doing—some quiet bracing against time, against expectation—finally loosened.

He had held her like this countless times before.

On dance floors that were too small and beds that were too narrow. In kitchens at midnight when the world had gone suddenly sharp with grief. On long mornings when laughter came easily and evenings when it did not. He had held her when she cried into his chest, and when she laughed so hard she could not stay upright. When joy made her light and when sorrow made her heavy, and always—always—he had known how to take her weight.

This was the same hold.

Different years. Same love.

Nan shifted slightly, closer still, and Mossy adjusted without thinking, his body remembering before his mind could intervene. Fifty years of small accommodations lived in the space between their ribs. He breathed her in—the faint trace of soap, the deeper familiarity of home—and felt the music carry them forward, soothing, calm, simply being.

In this moment, with her held safely against him and the night unfolding gently around them, Mossy knew—with a clarity so steady in its peace—that love was knowing how to hold someone, year after year, and choosing to continue to do so.

Across the floor, Walter stood and offered Maren his hand.

She accepted without hesitation.

They swayed—Walter's palm steady at her back, Maren's shoulders soft, her expression unguarded.

Mabel laughed as a firefighter—one with rolled sleeves and a grin that suggested he hadn't danced in public in years—bowed deeply and offered her his arm. She took it delightedly, leading him with the confidence of a woman who knew joy was nothing to be embarrassed about.

Rufus swayed nearby on his own, off-beat and unapologetic, arms loose at his sides, humming something that bore only a passing resemblance to the melody.

The ducks continued their gentle circuit of the pool, reflections of lanterns rippling around them. Pixies hovered at the water's edge—utterly still now, wings folded, eyes wide. Even they had paused.

Deadra played on.

Tears traced silent paths down her cheeks, but her hands did not falter. If anything, the music deepened—grew more tender, more assured.

Mossy felt the music move through him—through everyone.

Firefighters leaned back in their chairs, conversations abandoned mid-thought. One man removed his hat and held it against his chest. Another closed his eyes.

Mossy had spent months expressing his love measured by effort. By planning. By cement poured and pools shaped and lanterns strung just so.

And here it was, moving freely through the world without his direction at all.

Love, it seemed, did not require orchestration.

Only room.

The final note drifted outward, skimming the water, rising once more into the night air before dissolving completely.

No one spoke.

Nan leaned into Mossy's side, her hand warm and certain in his. He bent his head and pressed a kiss to her temple—soft, unhurried, the kind that carried years rather than heat. She closed her eyes briefly, receiving it the way one receives a benediction.

The cello rested quiet again.

Complete.

Mossy drew a breath and felt the night turn.

That, he knew, was the moment when reverence gave way to celebration—when beauty, properly witnessed, demanded nourishment. Music had done its work. Hearts had settled into their rightful places. Now the body must be honored, too.

"Well," he said, straightening and clapping his hands once, brisk but delighted, "I strongly suggest that the time has come to eat."

As if on cue, the chef stepped forward.

The paella pan already waited on the long serving table, immense and patient, its domed lid beaded with condensation. Two assistants flanked him. Together, they grasped the handles and lifted.

Steam unfurled upward in a fragrant rush—saffron and

garlic, shrimp and chorizo, rice toasted just enough to promise depth. The pan gleamed beneath, a mosaic of color and abundance catching the lantern light like polished bronze.

The crowd leaned in.

Someone whistled low. Someone else laughed outright.

"Mercy," a firefighter murmured.

The chef beamed.

Servers moved in smoothly then, ladles dipping, plates appearing as if by magic. The rhythm of it settled the space—scoop, pass, serve—until food was in hands and the evening shifted from anticipation to pleasure.

Mossy's full attention was on Nan.

She leaned forward slightly in her chair, eyes narrowing in pleasure. The scent reached her and she inhaled fully, like a woman who had spent her life feeding others and was now allowing herself to be fed.

When the first serving was placed before her, she didn't hesitate.

She broke the crust of rice with her fork, steam escaping like breath. Shrimp gleamed pink and curled. Chorizo glistened. Lemon caught the light. She tasted, paused, then smiled.

She took another bite.

Mossy watched the way she ate—unhurried, casual. She sipped the Spanish red wine he'd chosen, the glass heavy in her hand, and closed her eyes just long enough to mark the moment. When she opened them again she laughed softly, the sound unguarded.

"Madrid," she said.

He didn't hesitate. "Exactly."

Their smiles met—quiet, knowing. A city, a table tucked down a narrow street, late hours and shared plates and the particular joy of being slightly lost together. No need to say any of it aloud. The memory settled between them like a familiar companion.

Nan reached for her fork again.

And Mossy, content beyond measure, let the night continue unfolding exactly as it was.

Across the table Maren leaned toward Walter, one elbow resting lightly near her plate, her posture elegant even in ease. She spoke as she told her story, hands moving in precise, expressive arcs—confident, engaged, and entirely present. When she reached the end, she didn't look around for affirmation. She simply smiled.

Walter had been listening with his whole body, shoulders turned toward her, attention unbroken. He nodded once, slow and sure.

Maren lifted her fork and speared a shrimp, holding it out without comment.

Walter leaned in and accepted it, lips brushing the tines with practiced familiarity. He chewed, considering, then smiled back at her—small, content, unmistakably shared.

His hand found hers beneath the table, thumb brushing the inside of her wrist in a gesture so habitual it barely registered as movement at all.

Jessie stood at the edge of the tables, phone lifted. She panned slowly. Lanterns swaying. Faces softened by light. Steam rising from plates. A firefighter laughing so hard he had to set his fork down and wipe his eyes.

When she spoke, her voice was quieter than Mossy had heard it all weekend.

"This," she murmured into the lens, "is what happens when love is chosen. Over and over. For decades."

Mabel moved through the gathering like gravity—felt everywhere, announced nowhere. She adjusted a chair here, redirected a platter there, leaned down to murmur something to the chef that made him nod and grin. When she reached Nan's side, she paused.

Nan looked up at her, mouth full, unapologetic.

"On your second helping yet?" Mabel asked.

Nan nodded, lifting her fork in demonstration.

"Good," Mabel said, and moved on.

When the plates were cleared Mabel clapped her hands once, sharp and decisive.

"Cake," she said.

A cheer rose before she'd finished the word.

The Queen Cake rolled forward on a cart draped in white linen, its tiers towering, iced in riotous swirls of purple, green, and gold. Beads cascaded down its sides in gleaming loops. And atop it all stood the alligator—upright, jaunty, top hat tipped, cane raised mid-dance.

Seventy sparklers flared to life all at once.

Light leapt upward in a jubilant crown, gold and white and wildly excessive. Nan startled then laughed—full and uncontained—as the cake seemed to ignite into celebration. The beads draped along its sides caught the sparks and flashed back in purple and green, the tiers glowing as if the whole thing had been waiting for this moment to show off.

At the very top, the alligator—upright, top hat tipped, cane angled mid-strut—appeared to bow.

Applause burst from every direction. Someone whooped. Someone else clapped overhead. A voice rang out, delighted and unfiltered.

"Long live the Queen!"

Nan covered her mouth, eyes shining, then reached instinctively for Mossy's hand. Her fingers slid into his, warm and sure, anchoring him as much as he anchored her.

Before the moment could settle into stillness, Deadra moved.

She crossed back to the cello with an ease that no longer

surprised Mossy, lifted the bow, and drew out the first familiar notes—gentle, lilting. Unmistakable.

Happy birthday to you...

The sound floated across the yard, light as breath. Conversations stilled. Chairs angled. Someone hummed along without realizing it.

Happy birthday to you...

Voices joined in, hesitant at first then braver. Firefighters sang, off-key and proud. Jessie laughed mid-lyric and kept going. Maren leaned into Walter, singing softly, her cheek brushing his shoulder. Mabel sang with conviction and excellent timing.

From somewhere above tiny voices chimed in, too.

"Happy birfday dear Naaaan—"

"Long may she reign—"

"Cake for the tiny—"

The pixies fluttered and spun, inventing lyrics as they pleased, harmonizing with enthusiasm if not accuracy. A duck quacked once, solemnly, as if contributing their verse.

By the final line, the song had become something less musical and more communal—voices overlapping, laughter threading through it, the night holding all of it without complaint.

When the last note faded applause rose again, louder this time, followed by cheers and the scrape of plates as cake was served.

Slices moved down the tables, hands reaching, forks poised. Sugar and spice and bright citrus notes filled the air. Guests tasted, reacted, reached back in for another bite. Someone groaned happily. Someone closed their eyes. Someone immediately went for seconds.

Rufus accepted his slice with grave attention.

He examined it first. Turned the plate. Prodded gently with his fork.

Then he took a decisive bite.

There was a pause.

Rufus froze mid-chew.

Slowly—very slowly—he reached into the cake and lifted the tiny baked alligator free, crumbs clinging to its sides.

He raised it high.

"I am," he announced solemnly, "chosen for greatness!"

The table erupted into laughter.

Mossy laughed so hard he had to bend forward, one hand braced on his knee, the other still clasped in Nan's. She laughed with him, shoulders shaking, eyes bright, leaning into his side as if this—this absurd, perfect chaos—had always been the plan.

And then—because Mossy was a man who believed that more is more—he stood.

"Friends," he said, voice steady only because it had nowhere else to go. "If you will allow me one final indulgence."

Groans and cheers mingled.

Mossy raised his glass, the rim catching lantern light, his eyes finding Nan's across the table. She quirked one elegant eyebrow—amused, curious. Entirely herself.

"Now," he said, voice carrying just enough to ripple through the crowd, "the grand finale."

Rufus grinned like a man entrusted with destiny.

He ducked behind the tent edge and returned with a coil of thick fuse cord looped over one arm. The thing looked less like party equipment and more like something salvaged from a cartoon factory explosion. He crouched, struck the lighter, and touched flame to cord.

It hissed.

Then sizzled.

Then began to spark—bright, eager, racing backward in a lively, unmistakably unrestrained line.

A firefighter squinted.

"Uh. Chief?" he called, with professional interest. "Did we, by chance, grant them a permit for... whatever that is?"

Another firefighter leaned over, shielding his eyes as the fuse crackled. "I don't remember approving a *rope*."

The chief tilted his head, watching the sparks zip along. "Feels permitted," he decided.

Rufus jumped back, delighted. "She's live!"

The sky answered.

Fireworks burst overhead—gold first, wide and generous, then violet that bloomed like velvet flowers, then white so bright it turned night briefly into day. Reflections shattered across the heart-shaped pool, water becoming light, light becoming motion.

Gasps rippled through the yard. Chairs scraped. Faces tilted upward. Someone reached for someone else's hand without looking, fingers finding fingers on instinct alone.

Nan leaned back slightly in her chair, color washing over her face—purple, gold, silver—her expression open and wonderstruck. Lantern light trembled against her pearls. Firework light danced along the silver chain at her throat, catching briefly on the small key resting there, as if the house itself were watching with her.

Mossy didn't look at the sky.

He watched her.

And for a moment—just one—everything held.

Yes. This. THIS.

And then—

Smoke.

A curl at first. Thin. Curious.

The edge of the party tent caught, flame racing along fabric with theatrical speed.

"Oh," someone said.

Firefighters were already moving.

One grabbed an extinguisher. Another sprinted for the hydrant, boots skidding slightly on stone. Commands flew. Practiced.

"Line here!"

"Clear the edge!"

"Watch the sparks!"

The hose was connected in seconds.

Water blasted.

Hard.

Too hard.

The stream arced wide, catching lantern light—and then guests.

Screams turned to laughter as people ducked and scattered. Dresses darkened. Jackets were soaked through. Someone shrieked as cold water hit their back and then laughed hysterically.

Nan stood, arms out, as the spray caught her full on.

"Mossy!" she shouted, laughing, hair plastered to her cheeks. "Your timing is impeccable!"

Water soaked his tux, the fabric clinging, shoes filling instantly. Rufus danced sideways to avoid the brunt of it and failed spectacularly.

Pixies—unseen—lost their minds.

Firefighters adjusted, redirected, doused the tent completely. Steam rose. The flame surrendered.

Applause erupted.

Someone bowed to the firefighters. Someone else wrung water from their sleeves and toasted anyway.

Jessie spun in a slow circle, phone held aloft, laughing openly now. "This is officially the best footage I have ever taken," she declared.

Mabel stood in the spray, utterly unbothered, hands planted on her hips, steam rising from her shoulders as she assessed the scene like a gardener surveying a bed after a hard rain. Muddy, chaotic, and exactly what needed to happen.

"Well," she said at last, peering at the soggy linens, the damp lantern cords, the firefighters laughing openly now as they wrestled the hose into submission, "we're already wet, so—"

She didn't finish.

She broke into a run—shoes abandoned somewhere behind her—and launched herself straight toward the pool with the kind of commitment usually reserved for childhood.

The cannonball was magnificent.

Water erupted in a glorious arc, soaking the nearest tables, sending ripples racing across the pool. Ducks scattered, offended but resilient. Pixies shrieked with delight, darting through the spray like sparks.

For one stunned heartbeat, the world froze.

Then Nan laughed. A full, bright, startled sound that seemed to peel years away from her all at once.

She turned, soaked already, hair coming loose, dress clinging, eyes shining. She moved back to Mossy, cupped his face in both hands, and kissed him—soft and certain, laughter caught between them, the kiss tasting like wine and salt and joy. She handed him her tiara for safe keeping.

"Happy birthday to me," she breathed.

And then she ran.

She kicked off her shoes mid-stride and dove cleanly into the pool, slicing through water with a grace that made Mossy's chest ache. When she surfaced, slick-haired and glowing, she looked younger than she had in years.

All around them, restraint dissolved.

Rufus whooped and shoved a firefighter, who shoved him back. Someone splashed. Someone else squealed. Jessie lowered her phone completely and jumped in, shoes and all, shrieking as the cold water took her breath. Maren laughed and splashed Walter, who pretended offense before retaliating with precision. Deadra stood at the edge for a moment, hands clasped at her mouth, then lifted her skirts and waded in, eyes shining.

Extinguished lanterns swayed overhead, dripping night and water alike. Champagne flutes floated past like abandoned artifacts. Ducks resumed their glide, untroubled, mildly curious.

Mossy stood at the edge, soaked to the bone, tux ruined, hair plastered to his forehead.

He looked at the pool.

He looked at his wife.

He looked at the enormous stone hippo at the edge of the pool, now serenely overseeing the disaster with baroque dignity.

"When in Rome," he said—and dove in after his love.

What Was Always Enough

The house was quiet again. The deep kind of silence that came when a place knew its people were safe for the evening. Nan felt it the moment they reached the top of the stairs—the way the air softened, the way the lamps glowed low and steady.

Their bedroom waited for them.

Nan moved through it slowly and with familiarity. There was no need to rush what she knew by heart. The rug beneath her feet held warmth. The curtains were drawn just enough to let moonlight line the edges. The lamps on either side of the bed were turned low. Mossy had always said a room should be able to breathe at night.

She reached for her pajamas, folded neatly where she'd left them.

Faded floral flannel. Pale roses softened by years of washing, the fabric worn thin in the places that mattered most—elbows, knees, the gentle hollow at her hip. They were not pretty in any conventional sense. They were perfect.

She changed without ceremony, her movements practiced and unselfconscious. When she turned back Mossy was already there, easing into his own pajamas with the same quiet rhythm. Plaid cotton—Ralph Lauren, clean lines, sensible comfort.

He caught her looking and smiled.

And there it was—the faint lift of his chin, the satisfaction in his eyes he hadn't quite learned to disguise. The sideways glance that asked, without words, *Was it good? Did I do it right?*

She had told him, of course. More than once. With her hand in his. With her laughter. With the way she leaned into him all evening. But Mossy had always needed just one more confirmation, one more gentle yes, as if love—even after all these years—still required reassurance.

It surprised her sometimes, that softness in him. That after everything they had built he could still be quietly unsure.

She loved him for it.

Nan crossed to the bedside and sat, reaching for the small glass jar she kept tucked beneath the lamp. Lotion—rosewater, light and familiar. She warmed it between her palms first. Hands, then feet. Slow circles. Gentle pressure. The scent bloomed softly, grounding her in her body again after the whirl of the evening.

Behind her, she heard the quiet clink of glass.

Mossy set her night water down exactly where it belonged —just within reach, close enough that she wouldn't have to lean. He paused a moment longer, adjusting it by a fraction, then stepped back as though completing a sacred task.

Nan glanced at the nightstand.

The photographs were there, arranged for memory. A younger version of herself, sun-warmed and laughing, her arm slung around Mossy's shoulders. Another—both of them older, standing somewhere foreign, wind in her hair, his eyes bright with discovery. A black-and-white she loved most: them seated side by side, heads bent together, the world clearly elsewhere.

He had digitized everything years ago—every slide, every print, every moment she'd tucked into scrapbooks with careful handwriting and pressed flowers. But these few stayed. Anchors. Proof.

She felt rather than saw him come closer.

"You comfortable?" he asked, already knowing the answer.

"Mm," she said, finishing with her feet and setting the jar aside. "Almost."

She climbed into bed, drawing the quilt up around her waist. The weight settled immediately. Mossy followed, slipping in beside her with the practiced ease that came only from years of sharing space. He reached for her without looking, his arm finding its familiar place, her body fitting against him like punctuation.

Nan exhaled.

This was the moment she loved most.

Not the celebrations. Not the attention. Not even the music.

This.

She turned slightly, resting her head against his chest. His heartbeat was steady, reassuring. She felt his hand move—thumb tracing the slow, absent-minded arc it always had, as though mapping her back by instinct alone.

They lay there in companionable silence.

Downstairs, the house settled fully now. Pipes cooled. Wood sighed. Somewhere far away, a duck quacked.

Nan smiled into Mossy's shirt.

She thought of all the ways they had come to this bed over the years—exhausted, exhilarated, grieving, laughing. She thought of nights when sleep came easily and nights when it didn't, and how his presence had always been the same: steady, patient, there.

"Mossy," she murmured.

"Yes, my dearest?"

"Thank you."

Mossy shifted just enough to rest his cheek against the crown of her head.

"Did you like your party?" he asked.

The question was soft. Almost shy.

Nan smiled to herself.

"Yes," she said. "I did."

He exhaled, slow and careful, as if he'd been holding that breath since the blindfold.

"It was wonderful," she continued. "It was beautiful. And it was... a lot." She tilted her head slightly, brushing her temple against his jaw. "In the most marvelous way."

"I didn't need the fireworks," she added gently. "I didn't need the spectacle."

He made a sound—half laugh, half surrender.

"I know," he said.

"But I loved that you wanted to give them to me," she went on. "I loved how much you wanted me to see it all."

She shifted just enough to turn within the circle of his arms, her hand sliding up to rest over his chest. She could feel his heart there, steady and familiar.

"What I needed," she said softly, "was you beside me."

Mossy's eyes closed as he pressed his lips briefly to her hair.

"I was worried," he admitted, "that it would be too much. That I'd missed the mark."

"You never miss," she said. "You just give more than necessary."

That earned her a quiet huff of laughter.

They laid like that for a while, breathing together, lingering between wake and sleep.

"You remember Madrid?" she asked suddenly.

"The Flamenco?" he said without hesitation.

"And standing up because there were no chairs," she added. "The way the night felt endless."

"You dropped olives down your sleeve," he said.

"I did," she smiled. "And didn't care at all."

"And Pamplona," he said, already grinning. "Which I maintain—"

"—was reckless," she finished. "You running. Me watching. Furious. Proud. Certain I would never forgive you."

"You forgave me," he said.

Paris came without being named—her shoes kicked off beneath the table at the tower, his hand warm on her knee.

New York—pressed shoulder to shoulder in the cold, waiting for the ball to drop, laughing because there was nowhere else to put themselves.

Germany—castles in the rain, borrowed umbrellas, damp hems, shared wonder and beer.

"You know," Nan said after a moment, "I don't think it was ever the places."

Mossy waited.

"It was seeing them through your eyes," she said. "Standing beside you while you noticed things. While you made meaning."

His hand stilled against her.

"And you," he said simply. "Without you, they were just locations."

No poetry. No flourish.

Which made it true.

Nan closed her eyes, the words settling deep and easy. She pressed her forehead lightly against his chest, exactly where it had belonged for fifty years.

Outside, the night released its last held breath.

Inside, love rested—fully.

When the House Is Satisfied

The chair held Mossy the way old furniture does—as though it had always known he would come back eventually. He wore a lightweight cardigan, soft at the elbows, the kind that existed for mornings like this. The newspaper sat folded just so in his lap, though he had been reading the same paragraph for some time without progressing beyond it. A cup of coffee steamed gently on the side table beside him, poured into Blue Willow china that had survived decades of breakfasts.

Pixies drifted lazily through the parlor.

They floated, looping gently through shafts of morning light, wings humming at a lower pitch than usual. Bitter reclined upside down along the curtain rod, hands folded behind its head. Neat sat cross-legged atop the piano, polishing something small and unnecessary with evident satisfaction.

The house was not buzzing anymore, it was humming.

Mossy felt it in his chest the way one feels a well-tuned instrument nearby. The lingering resonance of laughter and music and too much food had settled into something steadier now. Contentment had weight. It had presence.

Nan moved through the parlor with practiced ease, gathering breakfast plates with the quiet efficiency of someone who knew where every sound landed. Dishes stacked neatly in her hands, porcelain kissing porcelain with soft, familiar clinks. She paused occasionally to rearrange the daffodil bouquets that had migrated overnight from outside to in.

The flowers were everywhere.

Yellow faces turned toward the light. Purple ribbon still looped around some of the stems, curling lazily where it had come undone. *Joyful debris*, Mossy thought. Evidence of a night that had been lived fully.

Sunlight filtered through the lace curtains at a gentler angle than the day before. Yesterday's light had been bold, theatrical—lantern-ready. Today's was forgiving. It softened corners. It smoothed surfaces. It invited people to move slowly.

From upstairs came the faint but unmistakable sounds of departure: drawers sliding shut, suitcase wheels bumping softly against baseboards, the zip of fabric closing around carefully folded lives. Voices murmured in the hallway. The cadence of people transitioning back into themselves.

Nan set the stack of plates down and glanced toward the staircase.

"No Rufus this morning?" she asked lightly, reaching for a linen cloth.

Mossy didn't look up from the newspaper. "Rufus," he said, considering the word as if it were a philosophical problem, "after a party like that, is either asleep or already defeating an opponent at pickleball."

Nan laughed, the sound brief and warm. "My money is on the pickleball game."

She wiped the table, slow and thorough, then gathered a stray napkin and tucked it into the laundry basket with care.

Her movements had a looseness to them, a softness Mossy recognized.

"And Mabel?" he asked, finally setting the paper aside.

Nan tilted her head, considering. "After all the work she put in?" she said. "I wouldn't be surprised if she slept for a week."

Mossy nodded warmly. "She was integral to the success of the party. To Mabel." He raised his coffee cup in salute.

"Indeed," Nan agreed.

They shared a look over the table—one of those unspoken understandings that came from years of shared labor and shared rest. The knowledge that some exhaustion was holy. That some effort deserved silence afterward.

Mossy rose and crossed to the window, coffee cup warming his hand. Outside, the yard bore the soft aftermath of celebration. Chairs had been gathered and stacked. Lantern cords hung loose but tidy. The heart-shaped pool lay calm now, its surface smooth and reflective, ducks drifting through it with the serene authority of creatures who had decided this was their domain and would remain so until further notice.

Beyond the gate, a line of black cars waited.

The world had arrived to collect.

Guests would leave carrying laughter in their pockets, rest in their shoulders, something unnamed but altered in the way they stood and spoke and moved. The house had done its work. It always did when given the chance.

Nan joined him at the window, slipping her hand into his.

"Well," she said softly. "We did it."

Mossy smiled, watching the sunlight catch on the daffodils, the glass, the water beyond. "Yes," he said. "We did."

Jessie was the first to come down the stairs.

Mossy heard her before he saw her—the familiar rhythm of quick steps tempered now by something gentler. When she appeared in the parlor she had her bag slung over one shoulder and her phone already in hand, lens awake and waiting. But instead of lifting it immediately, she stopped short when she saw Nan.

"Oh," Jessie said, and the word wasn't for the camera.

She crossed the room in three strides and wrapped Nan in a hug that was warm and uncalculated. Nan returned it without hesitation, one hand pressing lightly between Jessie's shoulders.

"Thank you," Jessie said softly into Nan's shoulder. "I had such a wonderful time."

Only after that did Jessie step back and lift the phone.

She filmed slowly now. The parlor. The daffodils. Mossy by the window with his coffee. The way the morning light made everything look forgiven. When she spoke, her voice had lost its performative edge.

"This place," she said softly, "does something to you. Put it on your bucket list."

She ended the clip without flourish, tucked the phone away, and smiled at Mossy—really smiled.

"See you down the road," she said.

Mossy watched her walk out lighter than she'd arrived, as though she'd set something down without needing to name it. The door closed behind her with a sound.

He turned back toward the parlor—and nearly collided with history.

Bithia and Cordelia hovered near the staircase, half-formed in the way they sometimes were when they didn't feel like making a full impression. Cordelia had her hands clasped behind her back, expression sharp but satisfied, eyes already cataloging the state of the room.

"Well," Cordelia said briskly, "the logistics were questionable, the execution enthusiastic, and the outcome—" She paused, lips thinning. "Acceptable."

Bithia smiled at that, her presence warm as ever. "The house seems...pleased," she said gently.

Mossy blinked.

They were gone.

Or perhaps they hadn't been there at all.

He frowned slightly, then shook his head and took a sip of coffee. The morning had that kind of quality—thin places, where certainty gave way to something softer. He decided not to dwell on it. Some things were better received than examined.

Footsteps again.

Walter and Maren descended together, Maren already talking, her voice animated, her hands moving as if she were still dancing through last night's moments.

"And then the music—honestly, Mossy, I don't know what was in that air, but Walter hasn't stopped smiling since," she said, glancing back at her husband with a grin. "He's practically humming."

Walter flushed, ducking his head, but his smile didn't fade. He looked rested in a way Mossy recognized immediately—not just rested but restored.

Mossy stepped forward and clapped him on the shoulder. "Well done, sir."

"Well done to you," he said. "That was quite a party."

They lingered a moment longer—Maren chattering, Walter listening, Nan smiling at them both—before heading out to the waiting cars. Their voices trailed behind them, thinning.

The parlor grew quieter.

Mossy returned to his chair, folding the newspaper once more, though he still didn't read. Nan moved beside him, resting a hand on his shoulder briefly before turning to gather one last bouquet that had shed petals overnight.

Deadra descended the stairs with a single small bag in

hand. Her steps landed cleanly. Whatever had been buzzing inside her when she first crossed the threshold had found a lower, steadier register.

"This," she said as she reached the bottom step, offering Nan a smile that held no apology, "was exactly what I needed."

Nan returned it with warmth. "I'm glad."

Deadra glanced around the parlor once more, taking it in as though committing it to memory. Then she adjusted the strap of her bag, readying herself for departure.

Nan cleared her throat.

"I have something for you."

Deadra turned back, brow knitting slightly. "Oh—Nan, you've already—"

Nan shook her head, gentle but decisive. She crossed the room and gestured toward the corner where the cello case rested, upright and composed, as if it had never belonged anywhere else.

Deadra's breath caught.

"No," she said immediately, the word instinctive, protective. "I couldn't. That's—no."

Nan didn't argue. She simply picked up the case.

Mossy watched her hands as she did it—steady, sure.

Nan held the case out.

"It isn't mine," she said quietly. "It was never meant to be."

Deadra shook her head again, one hand moving as though to push the offering back. "Nan, I don't think you understand. That instrument is—"

"I understand exactly," Nan said, her voice kind and immovable. "It came when it was needed. It stayed long enough to do its work. And now it knows where it must go."

Mossy felt the room shift with the soft click of something aligning.

Deadra looked between them, uncertainty flickering across

her face. Then something else followed—recognition, perhaps. Or responsibility.

She reached out—not for the case at first but for Nan's hand.

"I forgot," Deadra said quietly. "Somewhere between lesson plans and practice rooms and trying to make children love something they didn't ask for… I forgot why I loved it. Music became duty. Then habit. Then noise." She swallowed. "And I think, somewhere in there, I forgot how to love my own life, too."

Nan's grip tightened—steady, unwavering.

"When I played," Deadra continued, her voice warming as she spoke, "something sparked. Just a flicker at first. But it was enough. Enough to remember that this was never meant to be drudgery. It was meant to be emotion transformed." She looked at the case then, eyes bright but clear. "You gave that back to me. I don't know how to thank you."

Nan smiled soft and certain.

Deadra accepted the cello. Holding it close, as one holds a sleeping child.

"Thank you," she said at last.

Mossy stood, drawn forward by the gravity of the moment. "May I help you with your bag?"

She smiled at him as he walked her to the door.

Outside, the last of the black cars waited, engines idling patiently. Deadra paused on the threshold and turned back once more, taking Nan into a brief, fierce embrace.

Nan kissed her cheek. "Visit us any time, dear."

Deadra stepped away, lifting a hand in farewell, then moved toward her car. Mossy watched as she placed the cello gently in the backseat, adjusting the case with care before sliding into the passenger's seat.

As the car pulled away, Mossy felt it—a familiar tightening of the air, a hush like the end of a held note.

He squinted.

For just a moment—no longer than a breath—he saw him.

Anton sat beside the cello, composed and quiet, hands folded loosely in his lap. His presence carried the unmistakable quality of something finished.

Then the car turned the corner. And he was gone.

Mossy let out a slow breath.

He turned to Nan, who had seen it, too—he knew by the calm in her eyes.

"You were right," he said softly. "He wasn't staying."

"No," she agreed. "He never meant to."

"Will you miss it?" Mossy asked, glancing back toward the parlor, the empty corner where the cello had stood.

Nan considered the question with care.

"I'll miss the feeling," she said finally. "Not the object."

She rested her hand against the wall, the house solid and familiar beneath her palm. "This place has always known when to offer what's needed. And when to let it go."

Mossy followed her gaze as it drifted upward, toward the far wall of the parlor.

One of the paintings—one he didn't remember hanging—caught the light strangely. Just for a second its surface shimmered, as though the image beneath the paint were shifting, waiting for the right eyes at the right time.

Then the light moved on.

The painting stilled.

The house breathed.

And Mossy, standing in the quiet with the woman he loved, put the newspaper under his arm and smiled.

Whatever came next, he thought, *would come when it was meant to.*

And when it did...

They would be ready.

At Christmastime, the Nettles Bed & Breakfast glows with candlelight, Dickensian cheer, and the familiar comfort of traditions carefully kept. But when the cherished Infant Jesus statue from Daytona's live nativity goes missing, the season is thrown into gentle disarray.

Mossy Nettles, already searching for meaning beneath the pageantry of the holiday, is certain something sacred has been lost. All signs point to pixie mischief—specifically Bumbles, whose idea of help often arrives wrapped in chaos. As the house fills with guests, preparations continue, and the pressure to restore what's missing quietly grows.

Yet the answer does not come through urgency or spectacle. Instead, it arrives through an unexpected act of generosity: a child's willingness to give up something beloved so others might find joy. In that small offering, Mossy is reminded that miracles are not always relics preserved behind glass. Sometimes they live in kindness freely given.

In **Mistletoe and Candy Cane**, pixie mischief, holiday

traditions, and quiet grace intertwine as Nan and Mossy discover that faith, wonder, and meaning often return on their own—right when they are most needed.

Also by Chrissy Chicory

The Nettles B&B Paracozy Mystery Series

- *Lilac and Cherry Tarts* (Prequel)
- *Hollyhock and Sticky Buns*
- *Wisteria and Wedding Cake*
- *Mums And Pumpkin Pie*

The Culebra Chronicles

- *Eternally Connected* (Prequel)
- *Unabashedly Chosen*
- *Seriously Challenged*
- *Increasingly Complicated*

Hallow Rising: A Spicy Appalachian Romantasy Series

- *Bound by Blood*

Ink and Verse: Cursive Practice Through the World's Greatest Poetry

- Volume 1: *Emily Dickinson*
- Volume 2: *Sappho*
- Volume 3: *Voltaire*
- Volume 4: *Dante Alighieri*
- Volume 5: *Homer*
- Volume 6: *Poe*
- Volume 7: *Twas the night before Christmas*

Lucid Living: A Gentle Guide to Personal Growth

- Volume 1: *Personal Development*
- Volume 2: *Finance*
- Volume 3: *Health & Fitness*
- Volume 4: *The Art of Play*

Chrissy Chicory's fiction and nonfiction books are available through Amazon, Apple Books, Barnes & Noble, Kobo, and other major eBook and print retailers—plus library services like OverDrive, Hoopla, and Scribd through Draft2Digital's wide distribution.

The Ink and Verse handwriting series is currently available exclusively on Amazon.

About Chrissy Chicory

Chrissy Chicory is a Florida author known for weaving magic, folklore, and emotional depth into stories where the unseen presses close to the everyday. Her work spans cozy mystery, romantasy, and magical realism—each grounded in atmosphere, heart, and the belief that stories are living things, meant to be felt as much as read.

She is best known for the *Nettles B&B ParaCozy Mysteries*, a cozy paranormal series set on the Florida coast and featuring haunted heirlooms, meddling pixies, companionable ghosts, and second chances served with tea and sticky buns.

Her other works include *The Culebra Chronicles*, a romantasy series inspired by the history and legends of St. Augustine, Florida, and *Hallow Rising*, a darker folkloric romantasy drawing on Appalachian myth, ancient guardianship, and slow-burn, fated love. Across genres, Chrissy's stories explore what it means to belong—to a place, to a legacy, and to one another.

Beyond fiction, Chrissy is the creator of the *Ink and Verse* handwriting workbooks, which celebrate classical poetry and the meditative art of cursive, and the *Lucid Living* series, gentle nonfiction guides to mindfulness, self-discovery, and intentional living.

Readers who wish to linger a little longer are warmly invited to join **The Velvet Teacup Society**, Chrissy's cozy reader community devoted to magical storytelling, shared rituals of comfort, monthly teacup giveaways, and gentle virtual gatherings. Subscribers to her newsletter receive exclusive behind-the-scenes glimpses, and early news of upcoming releases—all at **ChrissyChicory.com**.

Magic is all around us.

A Kindly Word from the Hosts

Thank you so much for spending a little time with us at the Nettles Bed & Breakfast.

I do hope the daffodils were blooming, the tea stayed warm,

and the music—well—behaved itself by the end.

This visit happens to fall on my seventieth birthday,

and I've been reminded that the loveliest gifts aren't wrapped at all.

They arrive quietly, in kind words shared,

and in stories passed along to someone who might need them next.

If you enjoyed your stay, I'd be ever so grateful if you left a short review.

Even a few thoughtful lines help other curious guests find their way here.

Think of it as a birthday card slipped onto the hall table—

or a candle lit in the window, just to say, *someone was welcomed.*

With heartfelt thanks,
Nan
(and Mossy, who insists on adding…)

"A birthday wish is best when shared—
like a melody remembered,
or a cake meant to be sliced."
—Mossy Nettles

You can leave a review wherever you purchased your book,

or anywhere you enjoy sharing a bit of cozy magic with fellow readers.

Thank you for reading—
may your teacups never chip, your music play gently,
and may all good things arrive right on time

www.ingramcontent.com/pod-product-compliance
Lightning Source LLC
LaVergne TN
LVHW010659110826
845149LV00014B/3163

* 9 7 8 1 9 6 3 4 0 2 2 4 7 *